ROUGH LOVE

VANESSA VALE

GET A FREE BOOK!

Join my mailing list to be the first to know of new releases, free books, special prices and other author giveaways.

http://freeromanceread.com

Rough Love

Cover design: Bridger Media

Cover graphic: Period Images; Deposit Photos: Kotenko

This book was previously published as Sweet Justice.

1

ILEY

The sun was high overhead and hot. Sweat trickled down my back and three days of dust clung to my skin and clothes. My whiskers itched and I had the mood of a poked badger. I'd been searching for the group of men who'd carried out a string of robberies across the Montana Territory over the past three months, but up until now, I'd had no leads and no luck.

But perhaps my luck was about to change.

Riding from Miles City to Billings to Bozeman, I'd followed the Sinclair's path of illegal activity to the small town of Zenith. I knew their ranch was just over this rise. That's what the townsfolk had said—that it was three miles southeast of town—and if I just kept the tallest peak on the mountain range in the distance directly in front of me, I'd ride right onto their land. The information was shared easily enough, for no one in town seemed overly keen on anyone in the family, except the one female Sinclair. They excluded her from their less than positive commentary, which seemed odd. The first robbery victims had said three men and a woman had held up the train, and the Sinclair family fit that description to a T. Sure, they'd given a good description of the perpetrators, but there hadn't been a match until now. I didn't care if the woman was a Sunday school teacher; if she committed the crime, I'd catch her. She had to be a wife or a mother to so easily participate in the wrongdoing without being considered. What woman would hold up trains and stages? What woman would be involved in crimes where innocent people had been killed? Innocent people like my father. I'd learned over the years, even from my own mother, that women were sometimes even craftier than men.

Being a bounty hunter these past ten years, I'd learned there were all kinds of people; mostly the ones I dealt with weren't the good kind. Their values were skewed toward the wrong. Their consciences, if they had any, were weak. So when I looked to the other three men riding with me, we pulled out our rifles from our saddlebags and prepared. The Sinclair family was dangerous and I wanted them, dead or alive.

PIPER

As I headed towards town, I was thankful that the brim of my hat shaded my face and neck from the blazing sun. The horses pulling the wagon weren't any keener on the journey than I was. It was one of those days better suited for lounging on a porch with a book and a glass of lemonade than carting produce to the mercantile.

Why it had to be done this day, I did not know, for my brothers and father had been absent for the past week, and I'd supplied Mr. Banes with cucumbers and squash from my pickings just two days earlier. But I didn't question Kevin or my father, for neither man had a tolerance for backtalk or dissension. It was easier just to remain silent. I savored the quiet whenever they left the ranch. No one nitpicked my meals or my cleaning or had me do extra chores because they were too lazy. Even Bill was picking up their poor traits. Just eighteen, he was steering down the wrong path with just our older brother and father as role models.

I frowned as I swatted away a fly. My father had grown cranky and irritable when my mother passed on, but that had been almost two decades ago. It seemed his broken heart had injured his spirit as well, and Kevin and Bill had grown up following his poor example. The townsfolk tolerated my family's surliness but seemed friendlier with me.

I knew though, that this wasn't a life for me. I didn't want to feel moody and cantankerous all the time like the others. I wanted to leave the ranch for...something. Often I considered just riding past town with the wagon, but where would I go? I had just a little money hidden away. Having grown up surrounded by men, I didn't want to shackle myself to a husband who could be just as bitter and resentful about his lot in life. A woman's choices in the Montana Territory were slim to none. Marriage was my only escape, but there were no marriageable prospects. Men in Zenith did not want to marry a Sinclair. And so I was trapped. Trapped with a family I truly didn't like, in a life where my personal values were tenuous at best given my poor role models.

I was pulling at the collar of my blouse, tugging the damp fabric from my skin when I first saw the men approach. There were four riders, their pace slow and easygoing, but they held their rifles at the ready. We were halfway to town, far enough from the ranch where I was completely alone. When they rode up, I slowed my wagon and applied the brake to the wheel. They circled, focusing their attention on my garden baskets and me.

They were all large men. Hats shielded their faces from the sun, but also from my clear view. All were dusty and travel worn; it appeared as if they'd come a long distance, not just from town. They were strangers;

I'd never seen them before. One man came beside the wagon so he was just to my left. Because of the size of his horse, I had to tilt my head back to look at him.

And look at him I did. From what I could see of it beneath the brim of his hat, his hair was sandy-colored and curled over his tanned neck. His square jaw was covered in the start of a beard of a similar shade. His green eyes looked at me with such intensity I shifted in my seat. He was not an amiable person. Every line of his body was tense from his clenched jaw, broad shoulders, muscular thighs, to his large hands holding the reins.

I responded viscerally to this man before he even said a word. There was some kind of connection, a powerful feeling in the air similar to just before a thunderstorm, when lightning sparks the sky. I wanted to feel if his beard was soft or if it would rasp against my palm. I wanted to see if he had a dimple when he smiled. Was all of his hair the same sandy color, or had the sun bleached the strands lighter on top?

"Ma'am," he said, his voice deep and gravelly. The other men were positioned around the wagon, sitting quietly even as their horses shifted beneath them, yet very ready to do...something.

I swallowed and found my voice. "Hello."

"We are headed to the Sinclair ranch."

My heart sank. These men were friends of my father. Of course they were. They had guns out and ready to use. They were dusty and dirty and unkempt.

Their demeanor was not in the least friendly or gentlemanly—besides the uttered ma'am.

"Yes, it's about a mile behind me." I pointed casually over my shoulder. "Good day," I added, dismissing them. I didn't want anything to do with so-called friends of my family.

"Are you a Sinclair?" he asked.

"Yes, I am Piper Sinclair."

At my answer, the man indicated with his chin and the other men dismounted. One stood by one of my horses' heads holding the bridle, gun slung over his shoulder. The other two began pulling the tarp off my vegetable baskets.

"They'll spoil if in the sun too long," I pointed out, but the way they were rooting around led me to believe they did not care one whit about spoilage.

The man who spoke, the one who seemed to be in charge, watched me as he climbed down from his horse. "Are you aware of the stage robbery near Bozeman three days past?"

I shook my head.

"Surely you've heard of the train being robbed south of Livingston several months ago."

"Of course. It was all the townsfolk spoke of for quite some time. I heard two unfortunate people were killed." When the men began tossing vegetables over their shoulders and onto the dry, dusty ground, I narrowed my eyes.

All four men shook their heads in clear disgust. I

frowned "Is there a reason you’re questioning me and destroying the vegetables I’m taking to trade at the mercantile?

"We have reason to believe that the Sinclair family is the perpetrator of the crimes I mentioned."

"My brothers and father are not hiding in the bottom of that basket," I countered tartly.

When the man searching lifted a black metal box from the bottom of one of the baskets and held it aloft, the leader said, "No, but the stolen money is."

"But...I mean...wait! That's not mine," I sputtered.

The leader dismounted and took hold of my arm. "That's correct. It's not yours. It belongs to the Farthing Stage Company, Mrs. Sinclair."

"I am *Miss* Sinclair," I countered. With his height, we were at eye level.

He glanced at me for a moment, and then continued. "Very well, *Miss* Sinclair, you're going to climb down from the wagon so I can search your person for a weapon, then you're going to help us in capturing your family members for not only robbing a long list of stages and trains, but for murder as well."

"Murder!"

"Murder," he repeated, grabbing me about the waist and lifting me down as if I weighed nothing. His hands began roaming over me. "There was an eyewitness to a woman participating in the robbery."

"What?" I asked, startled to feel his big hands touching me. "Well, it was not me! Is this necessary?" I swatted at his hands, as I'd never been touched like this before, ever.

He glanced up at me. "Ma'am, we don't take chances."

He explored my entire body, particularly feeling the shape of my legs through my dress as my bodice was snug enough where it was clear a weapon was not hidden.

"You aren't the sheriff or any lawman I've ever met."

He shook his head slowly. "No, ma'am, I'm a bounty hunter."

I tipped up my chin. "Bounty hunter or not, I don’t know anything about those robberies!"

Seemingly satisfied, he stood to his full height, keeping a firm grip on my upper arm.

The men now picked the baskets up, one by one, dumping the contents onto the ground until they were satisfied there was nothing else hidden.

"You said a moment ago that you knew of the train robbery."

I tugged at the man's hold. Up close I could see that his eyes were a deep emerald and his anger was quite visible. Anger aimed solely at me. "Reverend Marks spoke of the robbery in one of his sermons. Does that mean he's guilty as well?" I countered.

"If he has a case of stolen money beneath hidden beneath his robe, then yes. I am not concerned about this Reverend Marks or anyone from Zenith. I am solely interested in you and your criminal family."

"I am not a criminal!"

One of the men brought the small metal box around the wagon and handed it to the leader. "You can use any term you wish, Miss Sinclair. You are under arrest."

My horses were unhitched from the wagon and given a nice swat on their flanks to send them off. There was a creek nearby and ample grass for them to enjoy. I, on the other hand, did not have the same liberties or freedom. I spent the better part of an hour in the hot sun telling them about the layout of the house, where the windows were and the direction they faced. I told them the placement of the stable and the other outbuildings. They asked after weapons and where they might be in the home. By the time they'd formulated a plan to approach the house, I was hot and thirsty and cranky.

They were very thorough in their roles and seemed skilled at their task. If I were to ride into potential danger, I'd want to be just as cautious as they. That didn't mean I enjoyed being groped for weapons I did not have.

With their plan in place, I rode directly in front of the leader, my back against his hard chest. The other men approached the ranch from other directions.

"I could have ridden one of my horses instead of riding with you," I said, shifting, uncomfortable being so close to the man. His left arm wrapped around me and held the reins; his right held his rifle, loaded and ready.

"I don't trust you, sweetheart, so if your family wants to take a shot at me, the bullet will have to go through you first."

He was using me as a human shield! The way the animal shifted and swayed, I felt every sinewy muscle from the annoying man's shoulders to his thighs. I'd never shared a saddle with another before and having it be a man who I found incredibly handsome yet loathsome at the same time, was quite ironic.

Why did the first man who'd stirred feelings within me have to be the one arresting me for robbery and murder?

I squinted into the bright sunlight as Kevin came out onto the porch of the house. No one else appeared, but I knew that they were watching. I'd thought all along the men in my family weren't nice, but now I knew they were also downright mean. Robbing and killing? It took their impersonal and sour demeanors to a new low.

"Piper, I thought you were going to town," my brother commented. He cleaned his fingernails with the tip of a sharp knife, one he kept tied to the belt at his hip. There was no love lost between my brother and me. Now that I knew of his deadly deeds, I saw him in an entirely new light.

"Mr. Sinclair, you, your brother and your father are all under arrest."

Kevin didn't stop cleaning his nails, didn't even look up at any of us. "For what?"

"Robbery and murder."

"You have no proof."

"Actually, we do. Eyewitness accounts, plus the stolen money box."

"What money box?" he asked, then shrugged. "Search the place if you want."

"No need. The money box was in the wagon with Miss Sinclair."

"Kevin!" I shouted. "You tell the man right now that I knew nothing about that box."

Now he lifted his head and glared at me. "You brought bounty hunters right to our doorstep."

"I did no such thing! They stopped me halfway to town. You can be angry with me if you wish, but at least tell them the truth."

He sighed. "Very well. She's innocent."

"Your words won't make a difference. The evidence says otherwise. Surrender, Mr. Sinclair," the leader said.

"To just you?" Kevin laughed.

I heard a gun shot that had come from the other side of the house.

"Not just me," the bounty hunter replied, perfectly calm. I jumped a foot at the sound and my heart beat frantically against my chest. "It doesn't matter if you're alive or not to get our money."

"We're not giving up without a fight." With that, Kevin moved at a pace that stunned me. I never knew he could do anything quickly; he was such a lazy person. His gun was out and before I could do more than blink I was shoved off the horse by big hands. I fell jarringly to my hands and knees in a cloud of dust as the first shots rang out. All I could do was stare at the hard ground, stunned by the quick succession of events. I didn't even have time to get my bearings or the air back in my lungs before it was all over.

2

ILEY

WE RODE into town as a caravan of horses. Neither my men nor me were injured in the brief shootout, but Bill Sinclair, the younger brother, was dead, his body tossed over the back of a horse. Kevin Sinclair had a gunshot wound to his upper arm, superficial but deep enough to make him bitch and moan about it the whole time. We'd tied a cloth tightly around it to stanch the flow of blood, but unfortunately, he'd survive. His father, Harlan, was unscathed. Of course, he'd hidden in the house while his sons fought his battle for him. He showed no injuries, nor said a word, and both men's hands were tied tightly before them. If I'd had my way, I would have them hogtied and dragged them. As for Piper, she was once again in front of me, her hands unbound. She couldn't flee, even if she tried. Four men with guns were quite a deterrent, especially since she'd seen firsthand what happened to the one brother who'd resisted us.

"I'm surprised you flung me off the horse. I figured you'd protect yourself with my bleeding corpse."

I stiffened at her words, for the hit their mark well. I *had* used her as a barrier against dangerous criminals. I guessed the Sinclair men wouldn't actually take a shot at their sister, which meant I would remain whole. But when danger did appear, I pushed her out of the way, protecting her as a man did a woman, not a criminal.

"I think one dead Sinclair's enough, don't you?"

I felt no loss at shooting her brother. He was armed and had already fired a shot when I'd gunned him down. In my line of work it was kill or be killed.

She glanced back at her brother's body, rubbing her arms as if she were cold, no doubt thinking about her probable fate. She wasn't one for hysterics, but perhaps the shock of the entire day was keeping her fairly mute. The circuit judge would decide *all* of their fates, but she'd most likely hang. That notion didn't sit well with me. In fact, nothing about the woman did. When I'd heard about a female member of the Sinclair family, I'd expected a married, older woman whose unattractive attitude would match her appearance. This was certainly not the case.

Piper Sinclair was young, perhaps early twenties, and quite stunning. Her coloring was similar to mine - light hair and green eyes, but that was all. She had freckles across her petite nose and her hair looked soft and shiny. Her skin, well, it was peaches and cream and porcelain smooth. She was slight of build and trim of figure. Her breasts were high and well formed, most likely a tidy handful. I frowned at the very idea. I had no place being attracted to her. She was a member of the Sinclair family, and their daring, dangerous and murdering escapades were known all across the Territory. We just didn't know who or where they were until now.

She seemed clearly surprised when the money box was found among her vegetables and all but forced her brother to clear her name. He'd admitted she was innocent, but I doubted it. If she were living with an outlaw gang, she'd had her entire life with her brothers and father, to learn the art of deception. She could easily be a skilled actress. She couldn't, however, fake her beauty or her pleasant scent. I inwardly groaned as her floral smell drifted up from her heated skin. A sheen of perspiration coated her nape and her pale hair clung there. I imagined her being damp with sweat, her hair wild across my pillow as I had my way with her.

My interest in her was only because I'd been without a woman for some time. She was appealing, being so close and sweet scented. What conscious male could avoid getting a cock stand from such a situation?

Perhaps the circuit judge who would rule her guilty or innocent. Could he be impartial, or would he take her curves into consideration?

No, the idea of her swinging from a rope did not sit well. The pretty neck that I'd just observed did not need to be broken by a hanging. Was she innocent or intelligent and sly?

SHERIFF PERKINS MET us when we rode up to the small town jail and helped us lead the prisoners into the single cell. It was much cooler inside, the sun not penetrating the room's thick walls.

"Looks like a big day for you and your men," the sheriff said as he led the recalcitrant prisoners toward the cell. They were a sorry trio. Kevin favored his arm, the father looked almost weary and Miss Sinclair's posture was ramrod straight.

I nodded. The money we'd receive for all four members of the Sinclair family would be a tidy sum, well worth the months of hunting across half the Territory, as well as the long ride home. It would also bring justice to those killed, including my father. I wanted to know these culprits would swing for their disregard for innocent lives.

"Know when the circuit judge will be coming by next?" I asked, hoping it was soon.

"Tomorrow." He held up his hand stopping Miss Sinclair. "You don't have to sit in there with the others."

She turned to face the sheriff, eyebrows raised.

"Why not?" I asked.

"Because she's free to go."

"Free to go? Why the hell is she free to go?" I ran my hand over my beard.

"Her brother said she was innocent. Isn't that right, Kevin?"

I glanced at her brother, a man I didn't trust one lick.

"Yes, Sheriff, she's innocent."

"She had the money box in the wagon with her," I countered.

"She had nothing to do with any of it," Harlan Sinclair said. In his fifties, he was weather worn and gray. He didn't seem to be overly affectionate parent, his words less to save his daughter and more about fact.

"Are you saying she was a patsy?" I asked, stunned.

"Hey!" Miss Sinclair piped up.

Harlan nodded. Yeah, no love lost there. The woman's father had used her to commit crimes. Whether she knew about it was the question. "Yup."

"See?" the sheriff asked. "Look, I've known Piper all her life. She wasn't involved in this. Now those two," he pointed to the Sinclair men, "those two are guilty as charged. Just have to wait for the circuit judge to rule. As for Piper, she's free to go."

Miss Sinclair smiled at the man's words.

I held up a hand. "Now hold on here. You can't just let her go!" Miss Sinclair's smile faltered. "The witness said a woman was part of the group that not only robbed the stage, but murdered innocent people. I'm not letting her escape while we wait for the circuit judge."

"Her family said she was innocent and I'm a character witness." The sheriff closed and locked the cell door, Miss Sinclair on one side, her family on the other. "If you don't want her to escape, then you can keep her until morning when the judge arrives. I expect around ten."

"You can't be serious," I said, my voice dark. I looked to the other three men in my group. All three shook their heads and stepped back, murmuring about I should just let her go, but I couldn't.

I sighed. A prisoner was a prisoner, even if she wore a dress, and had pert breasts, and freckles. She might *look* innocent and the sheriff might *think* she's innocent, but I would wait for the circuit judge to decide tomorrow. I'd searched too hard and too long to let her get away now.

How hard could it be to guard one woman overnight? I'd frisked her earlier and so I wasn't in danger of her shooting me if she got the notion.

The man put his hands on his hips and gave me his lawman stare. "I'm very serious."

I sighed once again. "Fine. I'll watch her until the

judge arrives tomorrow. Where the hell do you expect me to keep her? My hotel room?"

PIPER

THE IDEA of spending the evening in the hotel was more appealing than the alternative of a lumpy, dirty mattress in a cell with my father and Kevin. However, spending the night in the hotel *with* the bounty hunter was something else entirely. I had been relieved when Kevin and my father had both had proclaimed me innocent and the sheriff provided a solid character reference, but did Mr. Easton believe any of them? No!

I was free to go, per the sheriff, but the bounty hunter intended to keep me hostage until the circuit judge came in the morning. He obviously didn't like me, which made me frown. I'd done nothing to the man and he'd made me out to be an accomplice to murder! Even the sheriff couldn't make him change his mind. He hadn't said so out loud, but it was more than obvious, by his job alone, that he did not stand for anyone on the wrong side of the law.

I sat quietly in a tall backed chair with my arms crossed over my chest and watched Billy Michaels, the hotel owner's son, deliver bucket after bucket of water and filled a hip tub in the middle of the room. He gave me a questioning look each time he came into the room, but said nothing. The bounty hunter—I still didn't know his name—helped by carrying water as well, making the task go twice as fast; he was quite eager for a bath it seemed. I tried to leave once, making it as far as the top of the stairs. The man's large body blocked my path.

"Going somewhere?" he asked. We were at eye level for once and I could see flecks of gold in his beard.

"I do not have to stay here with you." I tried to squeeze past him, but he just shifted his weight one way, then the other, to block my path.

"Actually, you do."

I wanted to stomp my foot, but I would not stoop to his level of pettiness. "My brother and father said I had nothing to do with the crimes."

He shook his head slowly. "Said two guilty men. We'll let the circuit judge decide tomorrow. I'm not letting you out of my sight until then."

"You don't believe me?"

He sat the bucket down, water sloshing over the top. "It's not my job to believe you or not." Coming up a step, he forced me to step back. Picking up his bucket, he practically herded me down the hall and into the room.

I sat and watched as the men went about the task until the tub was filled halfway. The cool, clean water looked appealing to my sweaty, itchy skin.

Once the bounty hunter gave Billy his tip and the

door closed behind him, he started to unbutton his shirt. While I was curious as to whether he had chest hair and what its color was, I blushed at his task. "I beg your pardon," I said in my primmest tone, my spine straightening.

His hands stopped mid-motion, then he sighed.

"I appreciate your maidenly modesty, however I've been on the trail for the past three months searching for you and your family and I want a bath."

"I'll sit outside the door," I countered, crossing my hands over my chest.

His sandy colored eyebrow went up. "Sure, you will. You have two choices. Sit and watch or turn your chair around and spare yourself the sight."

I opened my mouth to tell him what I thought of his *choices*, but he pulled the tails of her shirt free of his pants, making it clear that he was taking a bath whether I turned around or not. I stood, picked up the chair and turned it the other way. Sitting down, I stared at the room's wall and counted the number of knots in the simple wood.

The splashing was the only indication that he'd gotten in the tub. This was utterly ridiculous! I didn't have to sit here with a man taking a bath. I was innocent.

I stood and began to skirt around tub without looking at him, my eyes averted, but he stood to his full height in all his wet, naked glory and took hold of my arm. "You wanted to join me?"

It was hard to keep my eyes on his, for in my periphery I could see broad shoulders, a solid chest that had a sprinkling of sandy colored hair. He had narrow hips and below...oh!

My cheeks flushed remembering the feel of that hard chest against my back as we rode. I had lived with two brothers and a father, but none compared to the bounty hunter. His hands were quite large and he was quite strong. Would he be rough when he touched a woman or could he be gentle? Those whiskers...I thought once again about them and how they'd feel against my skin...everywhere.

"I'm leaving."

His grip tightened for just a moment as he shook his head, then angled it toward the empty chair. "Sit."

I narrowed my eyes at him defiantly and didn't move. It was a battle of wills, but I knew that wouldn't be enough. He had size on his size. Nakedness, too, for he was just as intimidating, if not more so, undressed.

I tugged my arm out of his grip and huffed back to the chair and sat facing the wall once again, yet the image of his with droplets of water on his tanned skin filled my mind.

"You may turn around." His voice broke through my thoughts minutes later.

"Are...are you decent?" I asked, before I did so.

"Yes, Miss Sinclair, I'm decent."

When I stood and turned, I took in his clean clothes,

the dirty ones in a pile on the floor. Dark pants and a light shirt fit snugly across his solid physique. His hair was overly long and appeared finger combed, yet still wet.

"Your turn, if you'd like."

I licked my lips at the idea, for I was sticky and dusty, but was instantly appalled. "I couldn't with you in the same room!"

He held up his hands in defense. "I'll empty the water from the tub and draw fresh for you. I'll wait outside in the hall."

I eyed him skeptically. Why was he being so nice, so gentlemanly? I questioned his motives. "Why are you doing this? I'm just a prisoner to you," I said, my voice bitter, repeating my thoughts.

"At first I thought you were ogling me in the tub, but I was wrong, you just wanted a bath."

His words were mostly true, for I was longing for the water, but I was ogling him as well.

"You'll give me your clothes to keep."

My mouth fell open. "You're trading a bath for my clothes?"

"You can't escape naked."

“I shouldn’t have anything to escape from,” I grumbled.

He shrugged. "Ma'am, you're under arrest for accessory to robbery and murder.."

"I'm not under arrest. I'm innocent. Everyone says so but you!" I tossed my hands up in the air.

"The only person whose say-so I care about is the circuit judge. Until then—"

"I know. I know." He didn't need to say the same thing again and again. The man was insufferable! I put my hands on my hips, then remembered my brothers. When riled, they only continued to escalate the fight rather than be bested by a woman. Perhaps the bounty hunter was of a similar ilk.

I took a deep breath and tried to even my voice. I replied as sweetly as I could muster. "I don't even know your name."

An eyebrow went up at the change of topic. "Wiley Easton, ma'am."

"Well, Wiley Easton, I will thank you for the kindness, but surely people don't really care if a person's clean or dirty when they climb the gallows steps, even if they are innocent."

Perhaps I could play on his sensitive nature, if he had one.

Mr. Easton's jaw clenched. He hadn't shaved while bathing and although he looked cleaner with the dust washed away, he still looked wild and a little dangerous. I laughed to myself at the irony of that. He was the one guarding me and I was the dangerous one!

"Bathing is a courtesy. Removing your clothes is a requirement until morning." He pointed to the bed. "Wrap the sheet about you for modesty's sake, but that's all you'll get. I won't have you escaping while I'm asleep."

I felt my cheeks heat as his gaze raked over my body in a way that made me feel as if I were already naked. Sensitive nature? The man was the least sensitive person I'd ever met—and I was a Sinclair.

"How do you know I won't shoot you with your own gun?"

He grinned. "You can try, sweetheart, especially unclothed as it holds a certain appeal."

TWENTY MINUTES LATER, I was settled into the tub filled with fresh water. I knew *that horrid man* stood on the other side of the door with my clothes. While I felt confident he wouldn't barge in and see me in my bath —he might be contrary but he wasn't indecent—it was still disconcerting. Wiley Easton was *all* man and he could hear every bit of my splashing in the tub. Why should I even think about the man when he was so insufferable?

I dunked down until just my face above the water, as if trying to wash off all my troubles. My hair swirled about me. At a knock on the door, I startled and sat up abruptly, wiping the water from my face with one hand while covering my breasts with the other. It was a silly reaction, for the door remained shut and one hand would not prevent the man from seeing me if he entered. All of me.

"Miss Sinclair. Supper has been brought around. You should come out before it gets cold."

"I will not eat naked, Mr. Easton," I called out.

I heard him sigh even through the closed door. "The sheet, Miss Sinclair."

Frustration at the man made me slap my hand against the water, sending a spray of it into the air. I grabbed the meager bar of soap and scrubbed myself clean with more vigor than usual. I dried myself then tugged the sheet off the bed and wrapped it about myself. While I was covered entirely except for my shoulders and arms, I had no underthings. I grumbled to myself about the various forms of impropriety. I would eat dinner with a strange man wearing a bed sheet without any corset or drawers! Not only was he insufferable, but he was no gentleman!

Once darkness fell, I stood staring at the bed. It was a good size for one person, but not two. I'd never shared a bed with anyone before. "If I'm naked, then you get the floor." I pointed at the hard wood beneath my bare feet. He sighed, but said nothing more as he blew out the lantern.

I tossed and turned, for the bed was strange, as was the hotel. Even sleeping naked was strange. It was the first night in my entire life I hadn't spent on the ranch—the first night I didn't lay awake listening to my family.

A knock came early as the sun was just coming up over the horizon.

Mr. Easton stood, stretched his back then opened the door. I sat up in bed and ensured the sheet was tucked securely about me.

There stood a man who looked to Mr. Easton, then to me in bed. He stepped inside, forcing Mr. Easton to take a step back. He was in his fifties with graying hair, a portly belly, yet a very observant eye. "It's good to see you again, Wiley."

"Sir."

They shook hands.

"I obviously arrived earlier than you expected," the older man's voice held censure.

Mr. Easton looked to me, then back to the man and held up his hands in front of him. "It's not as it appears. She's my prisoner."

The other man arched one dark brow. "Since when have you taken liberties with a prisoner?"

"Liberties?" Mr. Easton pointed to my dress wadded up on the floor that he'd used as a pillow. "I slept on the damn floor."

The man looked to me. "Ma'am, I'm Judge Appleby."

I introduced myself as I held the sheet in a tight grip over my breasts. Mortification swept over me being caught like this. While Mr. Easton vowed nothing unseemly occurred and I could agree with that, I did feel caught as if we had.

"I'll get this visit moving along. Miss Sinclair is innocent and free of all charges."

"What?" Mr. Easton asked, running his hand across his beard. "There was a woman accomplice!"

The judge nodded. "Yes, it is a woman by the name of Sheila Carter from Miles City. While she hasn't been caught, she's been named and have been given a solid clue as to her whereabouts."

Mr. Easton pointed at me. "She's related to the men who did the crime."

"She is, but Miss Carter was the...*acquaintance* of Mr. Kevin Sinclair and their time together was well documented by many witnesses in saloons not only in Miles City, but in Billings and Hardin as well. Kevin Sinclair confirmed this just a short time ago."

"What about the money box? Clearly Miss Carter didn't have the money box in the bottom of her vegetable basket."

That made the judge pause. "You are correct, but the Sinclair men say Miss Sinclair had no knowledge of the box. They were going to put the money in the bank. Mr. Gibbons at the bank was familiar with this arrangement, albeit an unusual one, to collect the money and deposit it for them."

"He didn't think it odd that the money was hidden among a bunch of cucumbers?" Mr. Easton asked, his voice booming.

"Poor judgment, to be sure, but they didn't want it to be discovered and stolen," the judge countered. "I'll remind you we are in a hotel with sleeping guests all around us."

Mr. Easton sighed. "Then why didn't they tell Miss Sinclair? Why make it seem so illicit?" He glanced at me.

I had no idea about the money box until Mr. Easton and his men uncovered it, so I couldn't even guess.

"Her family didn't want her to know about the extra funds, for then she would know of their wrongdoing," the judge replied.

"You believe this?" Mr. Easton asked.

The judge gave him a pointed look. "The Sinclair men have had a fair trial for the crimes they did commit. I have no reason to believe Miss Sinclair had any part of their wrongdoing. There's no evidence to prove otherwise. Miss Carter is still at large and is someone you should go after. There is a bounty on *her* head, not Miss Sinclair's."

"I'm free to go?" I asked, tugging the sheet a little higher.

Mr. Easton looked at me, considering. I wanted to gloat, but now was not the time. I felt vindicated and once I had my clothes back, perhaps I could hold my head high in town once again. Although, with three relatives guilty of terrible crimes, it might not be possible.

"Not so fast, young lady." The judge rubbed his hands together. "Now then, onto more important concerns. Where are you clothes?"

I glanced down at the floor at my crumpled dress.

"I see. Were you alone with her all night?" he asked Mr. Easton.

"Yes, Your Honor."

"I dare ask the kinds of improprieties that occurred."

His eyes widened as if surprised by such a question. "As I said, nothing occurred. I didn't touch her," he countered, holding his hands up in front of him.

"Then why is she wearing a bed sheet?"

"She was my prisoner and I didn't want her to escape."

The judge's bushy eyebrow went up.

"Have you used this method before?" the judge asked.

Mr. Easton rubbed the back of his neck and looked abashed. "No, but she is my first female prisoner."

"I imagine so," the judge replied dryly. "I have high regard for your character, Easton. Of your values. I've known you a long time, and you've been quite successful at your job and well respected across the Territory. While I think your logic was sound, it lacked propriety in this instance. I don't stand for improprieties and this situation is most certainly one." He held his hand up in front of him when Mr. Easton was about to speak. "Prisoner or not, a woman can not be treated with the same regard. You've given me no choice here except to spare Miss Sinclair's virtue, therefore you will marry her. Now."

"What?" Mr. Easton and I shouted at the same time.

My eyes widened and it was possible my heart skipped a beat.

The judge rubbed his hands together again. "I like marrying people much better than seeing them hang. Dearly beloved..."

3

IPER

I WAS MARRIED to a bounty hunter in a hotel room wearing just a bed sheet. This was definitely not every girl's fantasy wedding day. Some unions were done spouse unseen. I'd heard of mail order brides where they were wed by proxy halfway across the country. I'd heard of marriages of convenience, especially when a woman was widowed and had children to feed. I'd even heard of shotgun weddings because of an overeager suitor. None of these were the case here. Yes, it was a shotgun wedding, but neither of us was interested in wedding the other, nor had any type of true impropriety occurred.

He hadn't even kissed me! If I was going to marry a man because of my virtue, he could have at least left it in tatters beforehand. But no, Mr. Easton was an ornery, annoying bounty hunter with honor. When the judge pronounced that Mr. Easton could kiss his bride and he lowered his head to plant a chaste kiss upon my lips, I hooked my hand around behind his neck and pulled him in for a real kiss. At least what I thought was a real kiss, for this was my first. I just wanted to know what it felt like, having a man's mouth on mine.

His lips were firm, yet warm, pliant yet yielding. It could have been that we had an audience or that he was stunned at the swift change of events, but I had a feeling there was more to a kiss than that. For just the briefest of moments he settled into the kiss, but quickly pulled back. The look on his face when he stood back to his full height was something akin to surprise. No, it was more like stunned. I think I must have had a similar expression because in that one moment when he actually had kissed me back, it had been...something.

The judge clapped his hands together. "Congratulations!"

I just stared at the man, not sure how to reply. *Thank you* wasn't really an option.

Mr. Easton cleared his throat. "What of the other Sinclairs?"

I may have just been married and my brain addled,

so I was thankful to Mr. Easton for asking that valuable question. My emotions were so varied I felt like I had whiplash the time I was thrown from a horse. My family *was* guilty and I knew their outlook poor.

The judge pursed his lips. "They are guilty of their crimes and will hang."

My stomach plummeted and little black dots swam before my eyes. I felt a hand on my arm and one just above my breasts.

"Easy, Laurel," Mr. Easton murmured in my ear. I was picked up and held snuggly against his warm body, but I didn't care, didn't register much of anything except that my family was all going to be dead, and soon.

"Judge, I'll take care of her now. I'd say thank you for stopping by, but...."

I just looked at Mr. Easton's shirtfront as the men spoke.

"Yes, yes," the judge said. "I'm sorry to have upset you Miss Sinclair, I mean Mrs. Easton, but there was no delicate way to put it. You're in good hands with your new husband. I assume you will want to track down Miss Carter?

"Yes, Your Honor," Mr. Easton replied.

"Good day then."

I heard the door close, but didn't care.

Mr. Easton felt warm and solid, comforting and safe all at once. Odd, since I didn't even like him. He just let me sit quietly for a time. "Laurel, you have to know your family was guilty."

I thought of Bill, running out of the stable with a rifle in his hands, firing at the bounty hunters—and me—with a look of hatred and intent blatant on his face. I'd never seen my brother in such light, but perhaps I'd never known the real Bill after all. Perhaps I didn't know any of my family. They were liars. Robbers. Killers. While they hadn't been cruel to me, they hadn't been kind either. It hadn't been easy for me on the ranch and I'd wanted to escape the life there often enough. Perhaps I knew what they were like all along, but just refused to see it. Regardless, their illegal ways had caught up with them and now they were to die.

I nodded into his chest. He smelled good. Like pine trees and sunshine and something else, something primitive and male and very appealing. "I know. I mean...I didn't *know*, but now I do."

Tilting my head back, I looked into his green eyes, so clear and direct. This close I could see the stubble on his jaw, the sleep tousled hair. Before I had time to even consider his intent, he lowered his head and kissed me, this time his lips brushing over mine as if testing the feel of them. His motion was slow, the pressure light. I exhaled at the almost soothing touch and he took the opportunity to slip his tongue into my mouth. I gasped this time in surprise, his tongue plundering, learning, and laving me with carnal, almost illicit movements. *This* was a kiss? I never knew a man's tongue went in your mouth or that I would like it so much!

His body temperature rose and I was surrounded by this heat. His hand moved to my nape to hold me in place and I was unable to resist, for I didn't want to. I'd always wondered what it would be like to kiss a man, but this went above and beyond.

Eventually, he lifted his head and his eyes were darker and focused on my mouth, his skin flushed, his lips wet.

"What...what was that?" I asked, my voice breathy and soft.

"If I am to be convicted and sentenced to committing inappropriate acts upon your person, then I should...we both should...at least reap the benefits."

"But...but my family." He'd addled my brain with his kiss, but not enough to distract me.

He sighed, set me next to him on the bed. I felt cold.

"They...they knew the consequences, Laurel, and are probably not surprised by the verdict as you are. Remember, they *are* guilty. They killed innocent people. There's nothing you can do for them."

What he said was true, I knew it deep down, but it was not easy to reconcile. "Then we should just go on kissing and I should just forget about them?"

He shook his head. "Kissing, yes. Forget them? No. You shouldn't forget about them, for they're your family, but you should remember the good things about them."

I darted my eyes away. "I don't have very many good things to remember about them."

He ran a finger down my cheek, which had me looking up at him. "I don't hold fond memories of my mother. Sometimes it's all right to forget. Didn't you ever just want to do that?"

I pursed my lips. Just yesterday I wanted to drive the horses right past Zenith and keep on going, to forget my life, my family. Everything. "Quite frequently, actually."

He looked down at me and grinned. It was the first time I'd seen him smile and it was quite devastating. "Then my first job as your husband is to distract you."

The word *husband* had me returning to my senses. I pushed against his chest and slipped from his lap, tugging at the sheet to keep it wrapped securely about me, but it was big and unwieldy and I fought the material.

"Distract me? You were trying to kiss me into forgetting that this marriage is all your fault!"

His lips formed a thin line. "Do you think I wanted to marry you?"

I shook my head. "No! You're the one who refused to give me my dress. You're the one who made it appear as if we'd done...things. That man," I pointed to the closed door, "thinks I'm a...a hussy!"

I was breathing hard now, and it wasn't from a kiss.

Mr. Easton had the gall to roll his eyes. "No, he doesn't. He probably thinks you're corruptible and I took advantage of you."

"You did!" I countered.

"Then we should at least make it worthwhile."

"How? How on earth can you make this mistake of a marriage worthwhile?"

"Kissing and then some."

WILEY

My life had gone awry the moment I'd taken on the case of finding the train robbers. The price on each of the men's heads was high enough to fund a retirement on my spread, but more importantly, could bring my father's killers to justice. While the Sinclair men were going to pay for their crimes, this Miss Carter woman needed to be found. I would not have any one of my father's killers roaming free.

It had taken months of investigating, traveling and questioning to end up in the shootout on the Sinclair ranch. I was used to leaving my property, but this time, I'd done it with extra focus and zeal. I was getting too old for chasing men and putting my life on the line, but my father's revenge came first. At thirty-two, it was time to settle down and a woman to share my bed. I just had to catch a wily and dangerous woman first.

I had not expected to obtain that woman—a Sinclair—by judicial decree. One minute I was fitfully asleep on the floor guarding a naked prisoner, ready to collect my reward money for all four of the Sinclairs and get the hell out of town, the next I was collecting a wife. *A wife!*

I'd been so focused on her guilt, that she was a *prisoner* and not a woman that I'd let proprieties slip. If the judge hadn't shown up early, perhaps the outcome was different, but no. He'd found us in a compromising way, yet absolutely nothing had happened. The irony of it was that I hadn't even touched the woman or enjoyed any of the actions to which I'd been accused—and found guilty.

I'd been stupid to take that damned bath and to make her remove her clothes, but since I believed her to be a criminal not a *man,* I assumed that since I was a bounty hunter it wouldn't have mattered. Piper had been a prisoner, not a *woman*! But my judgment was clouded, for even at the time I couldn't help but think of her as a woman, a very appealing, beautiful one. Clearly, I'd been wrong in my decision-making. I was married now to a woman who I'd thought was guilty up until a few minutes ago. The sheriff had said she was innocent. The circuit judge had said she was innocent, even had a different woman pinned with the crime.

I ran my hand over my face. God, I was shackled to a woman. I'd had no intention of every being married. I was jaded to the institution and now I was not only wed against my wishes, but to a woman who was linked to a family of convicted murderers. I didn't have to like it. I didn't have to like *her,* but we would still be wed. No matter what I thought of her guilt or innocence, it wasn't going to change. So I should treat her as a wife, for the judge had legally joined us so I could do so. That meant I could strip her down and have my way with her, when I wanted, where I wanted and how I wanted.

Right now I wanted to rip that sheet out of her grip and see her lush body. I wanted to feel the weight of her breasts, watch as her nipples tightened as I played with them. I wanted to discover the color of her curls that covered her pussy. I wanted to feel the slick folds there, to feel how tight she was. I wanted to fuck her. My cock wanted Piper, not caring whether we barely knew each other or not.

There was only one thing standing in the way of making this happen. Piper.

She stood there staring at me as if I'd been delivered by the Devil himself to ruin her life. Perhaps I had.

"There's no way on God's green earth that you're going to kiss me again. Being married means nothing other than we're stuck with each other." She reached down and picked up her dress, shaking it out with more vigor than necessary. Searching the room, she found the remainder of her clothes in a pile in the corner. Holding it all tucked up against her chest, she opened the door.

"Where the hell do you think you're going dressed like that?"

She looked at me over her shoulder with those green eyes. "Now you're worried about me being naked? A little too late, don't you think?"

"You can't go out in the hallway in just a sheet!"

I stood to my full height and towered over her, but she didn't cower.

"Fine! Then you go out in the hall while I get dressed." She held the door wide for me to leave.

There was no reasoning with a riled woman, especially one wronged as greatly as Piper. My cock ached and I was downright cranky. I didn't want to be married to her either, but she didn't care. Hell, if she'd trapped me into marriage, I'd be downright livid. I couldn't blame her, but it didn't mean I didn't want her beneath me in a soft bed. Perhaps a day of riding would change her demeanor. I had no clue what else might do the trick.

"I will settle the bill, then we ride to Banning. If Miss Carter is to be found, we will start there."

"You want to bring her to justice?" Her pale brow went up. "With me in tow?"

"I want to bring the murderers to justice. *All* of them. They killed my father."

She gasped, clearly not aware who had been murdered or the depth of motivation for justice.

"And yes, I plan to do it with you in tow. The judge didn't offer me much choice. I assume you don't wish to watch your own family members die."

"Really? I saw you kill Bill."

I groaned my frustration. "Not everything that has happened is my fault. He shot at me. At you, too! What kind of brother puts his own sister in danger like that?"

She tugged the sheet up higher over her body and lifted her chin. "What *bounty hunter* puts a woman in front of him as a human shield?"

I could feel my blood starting to boil. How did this little slip of a woman build my ire unlike anyone I'd ever met before? I wanted her naked and compliant, not prickly as a cactus. She might be naked beneath the sheet, but I had absolutely no chance of stripping her down right now. An argument was no way to get her in an amorous mood. Hell, *I* wasn't in any kind of mood to fuck if we were going to continue to bicker. I ran my hand through my hair.

"Up until ten minutes ago, I thought you were just as guilty as your family."

Her chin tilted up but she kept her lips together in a firm line.

"You never answered my question. Do you *want* to see your brother and father hang?" I asked. The way she'd been upset by the knowledge of her family's demise, I assumed, but I did not know her mind. I could tell her answer by the way she paled and looked at the ground.

"Of course not. I never want to see them again. While they admitted I had no part in their illegal actions, they used me and only admitted to it because they probably thought it would give them a lighter sentence."

That was probably true, but the judge didn't seem to offer lighter sentences to murderers.

"Good, then Banning it is."

WE RODE to Banning in silence, neither of us interested in speaking. What was there to say? We couldn't speak of the weather or ask after our families; both topics were obvious. We'd reached an impasse in the hotel room and I had no idea how to get past it. I was hoping time and a little distance from Zenith might help, but as the miles passed, it seemed not to be the case.

The town was larger than Zenith with a bustling economy due to being a stop on the train line. While still a distance from my ranch, my travels took me here frequently enough. It was my intention to pick up Miss Carter's trail here in town, track her down, arrest her and exact my revenge. Then I could settle into quiet ranch life with the reward money, but one last bounty, one last killer, stood in my way.

I'd had hours to formulate a plan and I hoped to visit the local saloons and brothels later in the evening to learn more about the woman. Fortunately, one of the people I intended to question later walked down the boardwalk and made my evening slightly easier. Or so I thought. Ethel Murbridge stopped us just down the block from the mercantile.

"Mr. Easton, it is delightful to make your acquaintance again," she replied sweetly.

Piper stiffened beside me as she took in the other woman. Ethel smiled and looked Piper over as if assessing a competitor. Ethel was the complete antithesis of my wife, with a lush figure and hair as black as night. While Piper's hair seemed to curl, Ethel's was sleek and straight. Piper offered no outward indication of any kind other than a slight tip of her head, but her fingers dug into my forearm like talons. The last time I'd made Ethel's acquaintance we were both naked and in the upstairs of one of the town's saloons. She was a lady of the night, but did not flaunt that fact while out and about. That did not mean Piper would not recognize her profession regardless.

I inwardly groaned, for perhaps having my new wife and past conquest meet each other was not wise. Piper's anger toward me wasn't going to be soothed by this encounter. Hell, I doubted I'd be able to bed her before spring thaw at this pace.

I tipped my hat to her. "Ma'am. May I present to you my wife, Mrs. Wiley Easton?"

"How do you do?" Ethel replied to Piper, and then turned to me. "I thought you did not wish to wed. If I'd known you could be swayed, I would have applied more of my charm."

Beside me, Piper lifted her chin as she took obvious note of the barb.

Ethel's *charms* were abundant and very skilled. While I had enjoyed bed sport with her on more than one occasion, it had been fairly clinical; I'd needed the release found in a woman's body, but had not sought any kind of connection. My cock didn't even stir as I looked at her now. She was lovely and I knew what her skin felt like beneath my fingers, but the only body I wanted to get my hands on was Piper's, but she did not know that, and the chances of her allowing it were very low.

"It seems I found a way to ensnare her unlike any other," I replied. It was the truth and let Ethel believe I was infatuated with my new bride. As for Piper, I had no doubt she would unman me before the day was out for the comment, hopefully once we were alone at the hotel. "If you will excuse us, I promised my wife some peppermint from the mercantile."

As we headed toward the shop, I considered Ethel's value to me. As a woman, she had none. As a whore who might know the whereabouts of Miss Carter, well, a visit to her could be very worthwhile. She could be an excellent source for information and I would visit her later. No doubt she'd assume I'd come to visit her at the brothel for some bed sport, regardless of my new married state. She was that confident in her charms. I would use that to my advantage and seek the answers I needed while keeping my hands to myself. Now if only I could make my own wife as eager for my attentions.

4

IPER

USING MY BROTHER'S WORDS, Wiley Easton was an insufferable ass. He not only forced my hand into marriage, but in the first town we came to we meet one of his strumpets. She might not look one to the average person, but a woman had an eye for these things. Miss Ethel Murbridge was a little too perfect, a little too relaxed and coy with Mr. Easton. *My* husband. How dare she flaunt herself and her charms to a married man? Of course, when he'd had his hands all over her *charms* he hadn't been married, but still. Ugh!

Not much was said over dinner, for I was so mad I assumed smoke was coming from my ears. He'd looked at me once and I'd glared back and from then on he'd kept his head down as he ate his steak and huckleberry cobbler. It was a smart move on his part for I had no interest in seeing his face.

His handsome, rugged face.

I inwardly screamed again. How could I find him so attractive? How could I remember how it felt like to be held in his arms? His scent? His kisses? I hated him. I hated him. That was my new mantra.

When he saw me settled in the small hotel room and turned for the door, I hated him even more.

"Where are you going?" I asked. The sun was just about to set and I assumed after our long day we would be turning in. Did he intend to take his husbandly rights and take me? So far he'd been honorable, but did a woman want honor when she was curious about a man's touch and could legally do something about it? Even angry and frustrated with him, I wanted him to touch me, for no other man was going to do so.

"Out," he replied.

"Out? Where?"

He scratched the back of his head.

"Mr. Easton," I said, my tone a little tart.

"Don't you think you can call me Wiley? We're married now."

"Exactly. We're married, which means I should be given the courtesy of a more thorough answer to my question."

He looked down at the floor, and then turned to

look at me. "I'm going to go make inquiries about Miss Carter. Where I'm going is no place for a lady. Don't wait up."

My mouth opened to speak but he shut the door behind him. He walked out on me! I'd been stunned to hear that his father had been a victim of the crimes my family had committed, it gave insight into what drove him so intensely. They'd been brought to justice and by now had paid the ultimate price for their crimes. He'd wanted justice served and it had, at least in part. Miss Carter was still at large, still not brought to account for her actions. While I could understand his need to find her, he'd left me! One night would not make any difference in tracking down the woman.

I sat down on the edge of the bed in a huff. I didn't want to be a shrew, but really, it was our wedding night! I thought about Banning. Where would he go that was no place for a lady? I was going to find out. Rising, I went to the door and peeked out. I quickly shut the door behind me and went downstairs, careful to ensure I didn't run into Wiley. Seeing him through the plate glass window of the hotel, I followed him, although I kept a substantial distance between us. The main thoroughfare was several blocks long but it was impossible to lose him.

After two blocks, he crossed the street and entered a building. The sun had set low enough now where it was hard to tell from this distance. I approached and the sign above the door read Belle's. Surprise and hurt combined in my chest. Wiley left me to go to a brothel! He'd barely even kissed me and went to find another woman to be with. Did he find my kisses that repulsive?

This thought fueled my motivation, but knowing I couldn't walk through the door, for I would surely be removed, I passed the building and took the dark alley around to the back. There I found the back entrance, which appeared to be off the kitchen. Going to the door, I opened it and stuck my head in. Several women dressed in just corsets and petticoats or gauzy robes sat at a round table eating.

Before I could duck out, one of the women called to me. "Looking for a job? It's all right, we sure don't bite!"

"Only if you want us to." Another woman giggled.

I'd heard my brothers speak of such places, even of the women within, but I'd never been to one in person. I stepped into the room and shut the door behind me, all four of the ladies looking me over. I tried not to shift or squirm under their very thorough inspection. The room was warm from the stove and had a distinct smell of onions and cloying perfume. "Actually, no." I cleared my throat. "I'm looking for...for my husband."

All of them laughed. "Honey, you tracked your man here?" The one with the long blond ringlets asked.

I nodded.

"He left you at home?" She eyed me carefully. "Is there something wrong with you? You know how to please him, don't you?"

"Yes, ma'am, you please him well enough and he won't come a wandering." This was said by a raven-haired woman with the largest bosom I'd ever seen. If Wiley wanted breasts of her size, I couldn't compete no matter how skilled at bed sport I became.

"Well, I...I mean..." Heat flooded my cheeks.

"Are you this unsure in bed?"

For some reason, that question altered my mood. I went from unsure of myself and disappointed to downright mad. "It's our wedding night and he's visiting a woman named Ethel. Is she here, for I'd like to pay them both a little visit."

All four women froze in place. "Your...I mean...." It was the blond's turn to sputter. Then she grinned. "Take these back stairs here and take the, let's see, the third door on the right."

"Thank you," I replied with a small smile.

"You a virgin, honey?" the black haired woman asked.

I glanced up the back staircase and back at the woman, offering her a small nod.

"You want this man in your bed?" she asked.

Did I? Wiley's strong jaw and big hands came to mind, the feel of his hard thighs beneath my bottom, his kisses. I nodded again.

She crooked her finger at me. "Let Delilah tell you how to keep your man in your bed."

I glanced at the others and with their smiles and words of agreement, I tentatively approached Delilah and she told me some things, some things that had my eyebrows rising in surprise and my nipples tightening beneath my dress.

A few minutes later I was much more educated. Before I went upstairs, I remembered the reason for Wiley's departure.

"Ladies, do you by any chance know a woman by the name of Sheila Carter?"

Another two minutes later and I was sent upstairs, the ladies urging me on. As I reached the long hallway, I took a deep breath. Third door on the right. One, two, then I leaned in and listened. Nothing. What if I had the wrong room? What if some naked man opened the door? What if the naked man was Wiley?

That thought had me knocking. A moment later, there stood Wiley. His eyes widened and his mouth fell open at the sight of me. This lasted for about a second before he stuck his head out into the hallway, looked left and right, then tugged me into the room, slamming the door behind him.

I could see nothing of the large room around his bulk. "What the hell are you doing here?" he growled. His gaze raked over my body. "Did anyone touch you? You weren't pawed or bothered, were you?"

"You're worried I've been touched by another man when you're here in the arms of another woman?" I asked.

The man had gall.

I heard a feminine chuckle behind me and when I

stuck my head around Wiley's large body to see who it was, I saw red.

"You!"

It was Ethel Murbutter or whatever her name was. She was dressed in decidedly less clothes than on the street, but all the important parts were well covered. Compared to the women in the kitchen, she was reasonably modest in her attire.

"Honey, if you can't keep a man happy, he's going to look elsewhere," she said, her soft voice grating.

She was baiting me. I was well familiar with the concept, as I'd grown up with two brothers. I would not rise to her words, for I wanted to save all my anger for Wiley. As I spoke, I poked him in the chest.

"Out? This is your idea of out?" I asked, trying to keep my voice from sounding shrill.

He grabbed my hand and pressed it against his chest. His hard, warm chest.

"I told you I had to ask questions about Miss Carter. Miss Murbridge was a contact I knew here in town who traveled in the same circles."

"You mean she's a whore," I countered.

I heard an indelicate sound from behind me. Her feelings were not my concern.

"Yes," Wiley replied evenly.

"Did you find out anything of interest from her other than what her nipples look like?"

Wiley's head tilted back as if I slapped him. "Piper, I haven't—"

"Haven't had the opportunity to get her naked? I know you want to avenge your father's death, but this is not the way. You say you haven't had the chance to glean any information on Miss Carter? Well, I have. We don't need her." I angled my head in Ethel's direction, but didn't break my gaze from Wiley.

"Oh?" he asked. His voice was calm and smooth. *Everything* about him was that way. Why didn't I get his dander up? Why didn't he argue? "Why don't we need her?"

"Because I have everything you need," I countered.

His dark eyebrow went up. We weren't talking about Miss Carter any longer. "Is that so?"

Perhaps it was the anger that made me bold. Perhaps it was the women downstairs who'd inspired me to ensure Ethel didn't get her little fingers on what was mine. I may not have wanted to marry Wiley, but he was *mine*. If I had to stake my claim, then I would. I wasn't going to get any other man and if I had my way, he wasn't going to have any other woman.

Thinking of my little lesson, I stepped closer, close enough where I could smell Wiley's clean scent, see the dark whiskers along his jaw, and put my hand directly over the front placket of his pants. I'd felt his hard male member when he'd held me in his lap earlier, but now, beneath my palm, it was so much bigger than I remembered. That was supposed to fit inside of me?

The ladies downstairs had called it a cock and said I should stroke it, so I did.

"Piper," he groaned. Wiley's eyes widened in total surprise, then narrowed. His lips parted and a hiss escaped. Using my other hand, I cupped him from below, in the area I'd been told I'd find his...balls. I wasn't sure what the woman had meant, but they'd said to grope beneath his hard...cock—that's what they'd called it—and I'd find these two soft, firm orbs. With my right hand stroking up and down the length and my left hand beneath, I leaned in and whispered. "Do you find me so lacking you need to seek out a whore?"

I felt the broad head of his cock and stroked it as I was instructed, knowing I was doing it correctly when Wiley's eyes slipped shut. After one none-so-gentle stroke, his eyes opened and he stepped back. Reaching around blindly, he gripped the doorknob and yanked the door open.

"Out," he said. For a brief moment I thought he was speaking to me and I felt devastatingly hurt, but he was looking over my shoulder. "Ethel, I've paid you for an hour so go find something else to do."

I didn't look anywhere but at Wiley, but I heard the woman's dissatisfaction and she all but flounced out of the room. Wiley kicked the door shut behind her. His eyes had that predatory gleam to them and I stepped back. He closed the distance and I stepped back again.

"Wiley, I...."

"You don't think I want you?"

I licked my lips and his eyes dropped to my mouth.

"You...you did leave me standing in our hotel room on our wedding night. You did go to a brothel and seek out a woman you've had...relations with."

"I was working."

"What was I to think? You left me for...for *her.*" I pointed at the closed door. "I mean, there's no comparison."

He slowly shook his head as he took another step closer. "No, there's no comparison."

I hit the bed with the back of my legs and sat down abruptly. All the confidence the ladies downstairs had given me seeped away. I looked down at my hands in my lap and I let my shoulders slump. "Yes, I see. I can't blame you, for you didn't want to marry any more than I. If you're going to seek out other women, then at least don't flaunt it."

"You think I don't take our vows seriously?" I kept my eyes downcast and didn't answer and only met his gaze when he tilted my chin up with his finger. His eyes were dark, clear and very, very intense. "I assure you, I take the convention of marriage *very* seriously."

WILEY

My hands went to the buttons of my shirt, undoing one and then the next.

"What...what are you doing?" she asked, surprised as more of my body was uncovered.

"Taking off my clothes."

She'd been a bold vixen just a few moments ago and now she was the shy virgin. I'd been stunned when she'd grabbed my cock, even more so when she'd cupped my balls with her other hand.

"Yes, I can see that, but why?" She didn't look away but kept her curious eyes on me. This was a good sign.

"You played with my cock, sweetheart. Just like an expert. I assume you aren't one and in fact, a very innocent virgin. Who told you how to do that?"

She swallowed and that had me thinking about what she could do with that mouth. "The ladies downstairs."

I clenched my jaw at what she'd done. "The ladies downstairs?" I repeated. "Sweetheart, we're going to talk about how a lady isn't supposed to wander a strange town alone at night, let alone enter a brothel. But not now." I stripped the shirt off my arms and dropped it to the floor. I sat down beside her. "Come here, Piper." My voice was level and even.

I would fuck her now as she'd all but taunted me into it. She'd been standing there when I opened the door, all bravado and sass. She'd come to stake her claim and if that hadn't made me rock hard, I didn't know what could. Besides it being ridiculously dangerous, it was hot as hell. Then she'd stood up to Ethel and had the audacity to grab my cock. Not just grab it, but fondle it in the most expert of ways. Then she'd had the ridiculous notion that I didn't want her, that I wanted Ethel instead.

I hadn't told her I wanted her; we'd only kissed and that had been brief. What we had between us was simmering, simmering as anger, but there was definitely lust there as well. We might be angry about the basis for our marriage, but there was no mistaking any longer the need in both of us. She'd started it when she followed me out of the hotel room, but I would take over and finish this. She might have a bold streak in her, but it was gone now. She needed me to take the lead, to be in control.

Taking off my shirt was just the start. I knew what I *wanted* to do, but not what I *should* do. We really were complete strangers and she was a virgin. While she'd been extremely forward and bold only a few moments earlier, it wasn't really Piper. She may have been given some tips from some ladies downstairs, she couldn't have learned everything. No, teaching her everything was my job.

I couldn't just toss her on the bed, rip the dress from her body and take her, at least not the first time. She needed wooing and a gentle touch, but 'gentle' was not a word ever used in association with me. My life was rough, my body was hard and big, my touch most likely aggressive. It would be difficult to control, for I wanted her readily enough, especially the way she was ogling my chest. My body, my cock, was primed and ready to sink into her. She would be tight and hot and I would ensure that she was wet and eager for me.

She stood before me at a pace so obscenely slow it took all my willpower not to reach out and grab her. "We're practically strangers," she said.

"That is about to change." Finally, I put my hands on her hips, her body warm and lush beneath my palms, pulling her into the space between my wide set knees. Her covered breasts were in direct alignment with my eyes and I stifled a groan at how, if I just lifted a hand, I could cup one soft globe and test it's weight.

"Here? In a brothel?" she asked, looking around. It was a whore's bedroom, not the perfect place for our wedding night, but I was not waiting another minute to get my hands on her.

"Definitely here. When I make you scream your pleasure, no one will care."

"Wiley," she replied, her cheeks flushing prettily. Oh, she was definitely a virgin.

The sound of my name in her soft voice was very appealing. I took her small hands in mine and brought them to my chest. "Don't lose all that boldness now, sweetheart. Touch me."

Her gaze flicked up from our merged hands to meet my eyes. I saw trepidation and curiosity in the green depths. She licked her lips and this time, I did groan. I couldn't help the sound from escaping. Nor could I help it when I put my mouth on hers. Her lips were soft and plump and unmoving. A sound of surprise came from the back of her throat. When she parted her lips, I took advantage and my tongue slipped past. Sliding one hand up her back, I cupped the nape of her neck and tilted her head to kiss her more deeply. I pulled back, just enough to talk.

"Kiss me back, sweetheart."

I kissed the corner of her mouth, across her lower lip to the other side. Her breath was warm, her taste sweet. "I...I don't know how."

"Just do what feels pleasing to you." I kissed her again, and this time she was a little bolder, her tongue meeting mine for the first time. It was hard to go slowly, to not plunder, but soon I could. *Soon.*

I kissed her and I kissed her until I felt her body relax, felt the muscles shift from tense to lax, her fingers pressing into my chest.

"Touch me, Piper," I said again. This time my voice was rough with need.

"I am," she replied breathily.

I shook my head slowly, took hold of her hands and moved them over my chest, my flat nipples, down over my belly and back.

Although her fingers were slow, she complied. The feel of her small hands on me had my cock pressing painfully against my pants.

"My turn." Carefully, so as not to make her skittish, I lifted my hands and began working the buttons of her bodice free. As I did so, her pale, creamy skin became exposed a little at a time. The top swells of her breasts were plump and full. I'd been correct in my guess; her pale skin was sprinkled with pale freckles. I couldn't resist and I kissed them, starting on the top of her right breast and worked my way across to the other. She was silky soft and her scent filled my nose. Floral, spring sunshine, and pure woman. It was a heady mixture. Her breathing escaped in little pants, making her breasts rise and fall as I kissed her.

"Wiley," she whispered, her hand tangling in my hair. As I continued to kiss her, I worked the material down her arms and over her hips so it pooled at her feet. One moment she was tugging me away, the next holding me to her. I smiled against her warm skin. I looked up at her from my very appealing spot, moving my chin back and forth, rubbing my whiskers against her, just above the edge of her corset. Her eyes were emerald green and a tad blurry, indicative of the start of her arousal. It was heady to watch her awakening to passion.

"Like that?" I asked.

"Can I...can I feel your whiskers?" she whispered.

I raised an eyebrow at her question, then sat back and tilted my chin up. If she wanted to touch me I wasn't going to stop her.

Tentatively, she ran her palm over my jaw, sliding it back and forth. She was focused on her task and when her thumb ran over my lips, I opened and took the tip into my mouth.

Her eyes widened as I sucked on the tip, then let it go.

"I shouldn't like this, but I do," she told me.

I couldn't help but grin, for it went completely against her earlier brazen behavior. She might have been mad at me, she might have hated that we were married, that I'd come to see Ethel on our wedding night, but she couldn't lie about her reaction to me. Mad or not, she was attracted and quickly becoming aroused. I ran my hand over her hair to pull the pins from it, letting the long tresses fall down her back. Then, I tangled my fingers in the silky strands and tugged her into a kiss as her hand fell to my shoulder. Her attentions were more ardent now, her mouth responsive. She was a quick learner. Shifting, I turned, bringing her with me and lowering her to the bed so I loomed over her, my weight resting on one forearm. I did not break the kiss, only lowered one hand to work the stays on the corset, wanting to feel heated, soft flesh. Once the sides of the stiff garment parted, I finally was able to see what her breasts looked like, felt like. Tasted like.

I sat back on my heels so I could look down at her. As I did so, she watched me, and certainly didn't fight me, her lips slick and swollen from my kisses. Her breasts were full and plump and pink tipped, with perfect nipples that I longed to taste. And so I did. I took one into my mouth, the plump feel of it luscious against my tongue.

"Wiley, oh!" she cried, her hands once again in my hair. I laved the tip, sucked on it, even grazed it gently with my teeth, testing what made her writhe, what made her breath catch and what made her moan. It was a sweet sound, full of longing and surprise and sheer bone-deep pleasure. What was so powerful, so heady about it was that I was giving it to her.

I moved from one breast to the other, licking and sucking and laving them while I plucked and tugged on the tight little tip. She was very responsive, and her breasts were very sensitive to my play. It was heady knowledge, indeed. I wanted to see more of her, taste more, touch more.

Her skin was so pale, her legs long and shapely. Everything about her was well formed and perfect. Running my hands over her, I discovered the inside of her arm was ticklish and that her skin was unbelievably smooth. How could she be soft and dainty when I was so hard and rough?

I stood tall, taking a moment to breathe and cool my ardor, but only a moment. I worked her stockings down her legs, removed her shoes, then her drawers last. She watched me with clear eyes, yet I could see nervousness there, perhaps a fear of the unknown. Hopefully, I was being gentle and slow enough to allay her fears of me. "Show me all of you, sweetheart."

She frowned. "I'm...I'm naked. What else is there to see?"

"Spread your thighs and show my your pussy."

Instead of widening her legs, she pressed them together and shook her head. "This...this is happening too quickly."

It was, but my cock didn't care. This wasn't just any woman; this was my wife. I was looking down upon the body of the one woman who belonged to me. While I'd earned the right to do whatever I wished with her via the law and God, I had to earn her trust to do so.

Sitting down on the edge of the bed, I gently ran my hands over her once again, gentling her as I would a skittish mare. "While it's true we hardly know each other and most likely will drive each other to drink more times than not, I have no doubt we'll be compatible in bed." Lazily, I circled my finger around the perfect swell of her breast. "What the ladies downstairs told you, I liked. Very much. My cock was—is—hard for you. Only you. We're going to be good together."

When I avoided her nipple, she arched her back and I watched it tighten before my eyes. It was all I could do not to groan. "How...how are you so sure?"

I shrugged. Meeting her eyes, I said, "Trust me to make you feel good and I'll trust you to tell me if you don't like something. I promise I'll stop. All right?"

I pushed my advantage, flicking the tip of her nipple with my fingertip and her eyes slipped shut.

"Yes," she replied on a moan.

Instead of having her spread her luscious thighs, I'd have to do it for her. She was of the mindset that if she did so herself, she'd consider herself wanton or forward. While I wanted her to be both, she'd have to learn her power over me. In the meantime, I grazed my finger down her body, circled her navel once, and then dipped lower and to where her legs were clenched tightly together. My finger dipped into her wheat colored curls and her eyes widened and her muscles relaxed.

"What...what was that?" she asked.

I took advantage of her shock and took hold of her thighs and slowly, gently parted her legs. My eyes widened and my breath caught at the sight.

"You look so surprised. Surely you've seen a naked woman before," she said, her voice tentative, clearly worried about her body and my judgment.

I did not want to even discuss the women who'd come before, especially since I'd just forced one of them out of the room. Their faces, their bodies all blurred together and were forgotten. All I could see now, all I could want, lay before me like a buffet and I was a starving man. My cock pressed against my pants in a painful reminder of what it wanted. I could see her pretty pink folds barely hidden by pale curls. Her hips were round and narrowed to a tapered waist. While trim, she was lush and soft and perfectly formed.

"You're mine, Piper. That's the difference. I'm seeing my wife's body for the first time."

She offered me a shy smile and flushed a pretty pink at my words. "This feels so fast, Wiley. Is it always this way?"

I thought of how I'd often felt lust and eagerness to fuck before, but this was different. *She* was different. I felt almost reverent toward her, even though we'd been wed barely fifteen minutes. I paused. It *was* fast. It was *never* this way and it was a little scary for me as well.

I shook my head as I stroked her soft skin. "No. It's never been like this before."

I would take it slow if it killed me.

"Don't I get to see you as well?" She bit her lip at her forward question.

I grinned as I arched a brow. "You want to see me, sweetheart?"

At her nod, I stood, tugged off my pants and let them drop to the floor.

Her eyes widened at the sight of me and she came up onto her elbows.

"You're...um...you're big."

"You felt how hard I was." I looked down at my cock that pointed straight at her, long and thick, the large head broad with clear fluid seeping from the tip. "Ever seen a cock before?"

She shook her head as her teeth bit into her plump lower lip. "Nothing like that."

"Explain," I practically growled. "What man's cock have you seen?"

She rolled her eyes at me and I felt ire at her lackadaisical attitude about something so important. What man had come before? "I saw my brothers when we were small, for the only way we bathed in the summer was if we stripped down and swam in the pond. But they were boys and you're...."

Her eyes were focused solely on my cock as she spoke, and widened when it grew impossibly larger once I realized I truly was her first.

"I'm all man, sweetheart."

"I've heard that's supposed to fit inside me, but I must have heard wrong, for surely you're too large."

"I'm glad you're pleased with my cock, but don't worry, I'll fit. Perhaps I should check though, to see?"

She frowned. "Check?"

I lowered myself to my knees on the floor, grabbed her ankles and abruptly tugged her so that her ass was at the side of the bed. She cried out in surprise. Placing one, then the other leg over my shoulders, I had the perfect view of her pussy. I didn't dawdle, for surely Piper's mind would forget about being surprised and decide to become modest, and I ran a thick finger through her pale curls, then brushing over her pale pink lips.

"Wiley! What are you doing?"

She was still propped up on her elbows and she tried to pull her legs back, but couldn't. My shoulders were too broad and my palm on one inner thigh kept her wide open for me.

"Making sure I'll fit."

"By touching me there?"

I looked up her body at her. It was hard to focus on her surprised expression when her nipples were in my view as well. They were tight and furled and I wanted to taste them again. But there was another place on her body I wanted to taste first.

"Remember, trust me in this and I'll trust you to tell me if you don't like it, but I promise you, you'll love it."

I didn't give her time to argue. Using both hands, I parted her folds with my thumbs, opening her up so I could see all her treasures. At the top of her pussy was her pink pearl, all swollen and ready. Lower was her untried opening, the first hints of her arousal making it shiny and slick beneath by finger. I worked a fingertip just inside and began to play as I took in the rest of her. Below her perfect pussy was her back entrance, tightly furled and closed. I knew that she'd be sensitive there; any woman who was so responsive to nipple play would most certainly enjoy ass play as well. In due time. We had the rest of our lives. For now, I savored the sight of her, the feel of her hot pussy as it clenched down on my finger. She was so tight; once I was sunk balls deep into her, there was no doubt I'd fit within her like a hand in a glove.

I groaned as her inner walls milked my finger, as if trying to pull it in deeper. I obliged and Piper's hips arched up off the bed as I did so.

"Oh my," she cried, eyes closed. She'd fallen onto

her back and her entire body was relaxed, yet tense at the same time. "Do that again, please."

I didn't delay. If she wanted me to finger her, I would do so. Her arousal made her wet and slick, the sound of it filling the room. I slowly slid my digit in an out, mimicking what would come later with my cock. I added a second finger, scissoring them to prepare her for she was so incredibly snug.

She hissed. "Wiley, I feel so open."

"Not yet, sweetheart, but soon. Soon you'll be split wide. It's time to come. I want to see you find your first pleasure. Scream as loud as you want. I want to hear it. I want to taste it."

"Taste it?"

Instead of answering her, I showed her what I meant as I lowered my head to lick over her damp flesh. Her taste made my mouth water. It was sweet, just like the rest of her. My fingers continued to work into her, but never far enough to breach her maiden-head. That was for my cock. Instead, I found the soft, spongy spot just inside that had her cry out. Curling the pads of my fingers over it again and again had her writhing. When I combined that with the tip of my tongue sliding over her round little clit, finding the left side of it to be the sensitive spot, she came.

The muscles in her legs tightened against my shoulders, and her heels dug into my back. Her hands tangled and tugged at my hair. She cried out her release loud enough for the other guests to surely have heard her. I didn't care. I didn't care about anything except giving her exactly what she needed. But watching her in the throes of passion had my cock aching, weeping pre-ejaculate so it dripped down my length.

Once her pleasure ebbed, I lifted my head, and shifted my shoulders so that her legs fell around me. "Wrap your legs around my waist, sweetheart."

She was pliant enough at the moment to do as I bid without thought or argument. She would not be telling me to stop. When I felt her ankles lock at my lower back, I pulled my fingers free and grabbed the base of my cock in a tight grip.

"See what you do to me?"

Piper's eyes were blurry, yet focused on how my hand stroked up and down the length of my dick, her cheeks flushed and her brow damp with sweat. "You're even bigger." Her voice was breathy and surprised.

I aligned myself up to her slick, virgin opening. "It's time, sweetheart. Time to make you mine. This is for us. You and me. No judges. No ceremony. Just this."

She had enough clarity after her first orgasm to understand of what I spoke. I was taking her because I chose it, not because it was demanded. She was giving herself to me, gifting me with her virginity because it was her decision. We were agreeing to this hasty, mismatched marriage of our own accord.

"Yes," she replied.

With that one word, I nudged the broad head of my

cock into her and I watched as her pussy lips flowered open, stretched wide by my entry. She was so slick I didn't even have to work my way in, and I took my time to slowly sink into her. I felt her maidenhead, but it was no barrier for the eagerness of my cock. There was the briefest moment of resistance before I slid in all the way.

Piper cried out at the intrusion and clenched the quilt on the bed at her sides. Her eyes were wide and I saw a hint of pain there.

"I'm in, sweetheart. You took me so well. See? I fit."

She licked her lips and held still. "I...I'm not sure. I feel...oh, God, Wiley, I feel so full."

I grinned, knowing how well I filled her, but sweat dotted my brow and every muscle in my body tensed from remaining still. She was as tight as I imagined. Wet and slick and so very hot. She was heaven on earth and I'd just sunk right into it. Yet my cock was screaming at me to move, to pull back and slide in deep once again. Not slow nor gentle. Rough and hard and untamed.

"Getting better?" I asked through clenched teeth.

"That's it? It's all over?"

"Over? We're just getting started." I began to move then, not only because I couldn't wait another second, but also I wanted to show her what fucking truly was about. She was going to love it, I knew, and I couldn't wait to see her let go, to fuck with complete abandon.

"Oh!" she cried, eyes wide as I pulled back almost

free except for where her clinging pussy lips held me in place, before again filled her deeply.

"Like that?"

She nodded. I started to move then in earnest, letting my need take over yet watching her cautiously. I shouldn't have been concerned, for after about the third deep penetration, her eyes slid shut and her hips rose to meet mine.

"More?" I asked.

"More," she repeated. "Harder."

Harder? She wanted harder? I could deliver. My mind went blank then, for I couldn't control myself any longer. My pleasure built at the base of my spine, my balls drawing up and filling with my seed. It was hot and scalding and plentiful and I knew that it would fill her right up. Before then, however, I needed her to come again. I reached down and ran my thumb over her slick clit. It didn't take more than that for she'd been right on the precipice.

She was wanton and wild when she came. Every concern she had was gone from her mind. Her hair was a tangle about her thrashing head, her thighs clenched tightly around my waist. I felt her inner walls clench down rhythmically on my cock in a way that had me coming. It was not something I could resist; it was too decadent and hot and...incredible.

I thrust my hips one final time, filling her to the brink, then I fell over. I growled my pleasure as I gripped her hips. There would be marks there most assuredly, but I would consider them part of a virgin's claiming. Piper wasn't some breakable waif. She reveled and thrived beneath my hand, beneath my body and filled with my cock.

I fell forward, placing all of my weight onto my hand beside her head so our rapid breaths mingled. I was still fully seated as the last few spasms of her inner walls milked the remainder of seed from my cock.

The scent of our joining was pungent and strong in the air, the room warm, but nothing was as appealing as recovering fully embedded in Piper's pussy. I knew I'd have to pull out, but my cock stand had not diminished. I wanted her again, but my randiness would have to hold for at least a few minutes. I needed to assess my bride, to know that she was well after her first fucking. From the small smile that curled the corner of her mouth, the way her skin was flushed yet luminescent in the morning sunshine streaming through the window, I knew she was sated and replete.

5

PIPER

"WHILE I'D LIKE to stay abed for the remainder of the night...hell, the remainder of the week, we can't stay here."

It was the first chance I had to look at the room. It was plain, only a bed and a dresser, the walls painted a plain white. The quilt we were sprawled upon was a mixture of dark fabrics—blood red, royal blue and even some dark heather. It was striking and very bold, perhaps matching the personality of its owner.

Now that my anger and ardor had both cooled, reality set in.

"Oh God," I groaned, tossing an arm over my eyes. Perhaps if I couldn't see Wiley he couldn't see me.

Mr. Easton's—no—Wiley's fingers began to fiddle with a long lock of my hair, tugging on it gently. After he'd pulled himself from my body, he'd fallen to his side and pulled me into him, his arm and leg thrown over me as if trying to keep me from escaping. If he made me feel that amazing not once, but twice, I had no interest in going anywhere.

He was so different from me; the hair on his leg tickled my smooth thigh, his arm was corded with muscle and his hand, just simply cupping my left breast, was large and his fingers long. Our size difference was obvious now, for I felt small and dainty beside him. Remarkably, he had been gentle with me; his hands and mouth and even his cock had been patient and somewhat restrained. That was, at least, until I uttered the word *"harder."* That single word was a signal to him to unleash whatever control he'd held and then he hadn't been gentle.

His hands had gripped my hips tightly, and his cock had slammed into me as it rubbed and slid over incredible places inside that had my eyes practically rolling to the back of my head. It had gone from sweet to carnal in an instant. The sound of our joining, flesh slapping flesh, filled the room. I couldn't help the little sounds that had escaped my throat and they seemed to only build Wiley's intensity. Fucking—the word he'd used for what we'd done—was wet and dirty and wild...and I loved it. He'd been right to make me trust him, for he certainly knew what he was doing.

"What's the matter, sweetheart?"

I refused to look at him. "What you must think of me!"

He pulled on my arm, lowering it from my face so I could see the very satisfied look on his face. "That you're wild and wanton and very, very sexy?"

"Wanton, definitely. Brazen." My body was relaxed and sated, yet between my thighs, my flesh was hot and tender. Deep inside, I ached, a combination of the end of my virginity and being filled so completely by such a large cock. He was large; if he hadn't been so diligent in his early attentions I would have been fearful. Well, I had been fearful, but more so. I'd forgotten about the reasoning for our marriage. I'd forgotten about my family and their demise. I'd forgotten everything but Wiley.

"You're mine now and there's no going back."

True. I could feel his seed seeping from me.

"You're not bothered by my...boldness?" I asked, fearful of his answer.

"Your boldness in bed pleases me. Your boldness in charging into a brothel bothers me a great deal." Catching me by surprise, he easily maneuvered me onto my belly.

"Wiley, what—"

Smack.

His hand came down on my bottom and I heard the loud sound before I felt the sharp sting.

"Wiley!" I cried, whipping my head around to look

at him, pushing up onto my hands and knees to get away.

"Good, just the way I want you." He came up on his knees beside me and gripped my hip firmly. "Don't move."

Smack.

"What are you doing?" I squealed as his palm struck a different place on my bottom.

"Spanking you for your blatant disregard for your safety."

Smack.

"You went to see a whore on our wedding night!"

Smack.

"I was working."

"Yes, interrogating someone in just her underthings. It seems your tact is to strip her naked," I countered, thinking of how we'd been forced to wed in the first place. "Good thing you were in a brothel otherwise you might have to marry her as well!"

Smack.

"You are intentionally swaying the conversation from the reason for this spanking. You will not put yourself in danger."

Each word of the sentence was punctuated by a hard spank.

I gripped the quilt tightly as the sting settled in and turned to heat. After one last spank, Wiley smoothed his hand over my sore bottom. "There. Have you learned your lesson?"

I wasn't contrite, not in the least. While I found his point valid, his punishment did not make me reasonable. "Will you stop meeting women in brothels?"

"This brothel? Once word spreads that my wife came and shared her ire, I won't be able to show my face here again."

I narrowed my eyes at him. The nerve of the man! "You spanked me for following you to a brothel so no other woman could have you and that's your response?" I started to move off the bed but he stopped me.

"No, my response is this." He slipped his fingers past my sore bottom and between my thighs to slip inside of me. When I groaned, he continued. "I love that you're possessive and so my fierce bride shall have a reward. For while this pussy belongs to me, my cock is yours, sweetheart."

I arched my back like a cat, pushing my hips back into the movements of his hand, making his fingers plunge deeper. "Wiley!" I cried, knowing now how the pleasure filled me and filled me until I overflowed.

"My cock is yours," he repeated. "Of that you should have no doubt."

I glanced at him over my shoulder. He grinned, showing off straight white teeth. He was so handsome and when he smiled, it was almost breathtaking. His hair was tousled and he appeared quite pleased with himself. His was quite adept and both of us most definitely reaped the benefits. "From the look on your face, you don't believe me, but I think we'll both enjoy proving those words."

It didn't take me long to come again, this time I screamed and the ladies in the kitchen must have heard. While his cock had been so big and thick and filled me so deeply, Wiley's fingers moved at a gentle, leisurely pace and were able to curl and rub over hidden, secret places inside of me.

"Yes, it feels *so* good," I moaned, collapsing down onto the bed and catching my breath.

Wiley stood, naked and incredible looking, to grab his clothes.

"That scream certainly redeemed my manhood," he told me and I tossed a pillow at him. He ducked and grinned again. "Now we may leave the room."

"Oh?" I asked. I was content to remain abed, although my bottom stung.

"You wish to spend the night in a brothel, sweetheart?"

I shook my head from the languorous feelings that made me so relaxed and sated. I did not wish to remain in a brothel, especially when I knew Ethel would most likely be returning. While I might be wanton and brazen, I did not need another confrontation with the woman; Wiley had fucked any reasoning out of my head.

"I believe your dress is still worthy for wear." His voice was scratchy and rough, yet deep and surprisingly soothing.

"Why would it not be wearable?" I asked.

"You had your hand on my cock, Piper. I could not be held accountable for my actions in my haste to strip you bare and make you mine."

I climbed into the garment and began doing up the buttons, which seemed to be all intact, Wiley watching me the entire time. "One of these days I will not show as much restraint at the start," he growled.

His words had my inner walls clenching. "Promise?"

He came over to me and stroked the back of his knuckles down my cheek. "Oh, I promise, sweetheart."

"What did the ladies at the brothel tell you?" Wiley asked, taking over doing up the buttons on my dress. The feel of his knuckles brushing over my breasts had me losing focus.

"They told me how to rub your...cock so you liked it." My cheeks were on fire and I looked at the buttons of his shirt.

His hands paused which had me glancing up at him. "You will have to show me later. My question was about Miss Carter. What did they tell you about her?"

I think my cheeks reddened even further at the misunderstanding. "Oh, um...she used to work there with them, but left about six months ago. They couldn't say exactly, but it was winter. They believe she headed to Carey."

Once all the buttons were done up, he tapped the tip of my nose. "Then we're off to Carey."

WILEY

I SPENT the ride to Carey thinking about Piper and my cock pressed painfully against my pants—riding a saddle is not the place to be with a cock stand—and my balls ached with the need to come. I couldn't help but remember how she felt in my arms once we returned to the hotel. I'd stripped her bare once again and held her all night. I didn't touch her nor make any forward advances. She had to have been sore from having her maidenhead torn and I hadn't been gentle. While she'd readily enjoyed herself, coming not once but twice, she was unused to my cock and such vigorous attentions. When I'd slipped my fingers into her after I spanked her, she'd been so incredibly tight. I'd been careful and tried to be gentle as I made her come because of the telling sign of her virgin blood and my seed coating my fingers.

It had taken all my willpower not to take her in the tall grasses as we let the horses drink from a nearby creek. I'd fought the urge to pull her toward me as we rode side by side to kiss her. I'd struggled to just...wait.

The sky was a mixture of clouds and sun, making the air cooler than the day before. We were alone on the vast prairie, the sound of the wind blowing through the tall grass the only sound. "Tonight I will search the brothels for Miss Carter."

Her posture stiffened even more. How she could ride in that confounded corset and breathe was beyond me. "Do you really need to go to another brothel?"

My eyebrows went up beneath my hat. "Oh? Don't trust me, sweetheart?"

She turned to look at me, her face shadowed beneath her bonnet. "We barely know each other."

I grinned. "I know what color your nipples are. I know what you sound like when you come. I know how tight your pussy is. I know what you taste like."

She flushed prettily. "That is not what I meant and you know it," she replied primly. "How would you feel if I went into a saloon to find a man that was wanted."?

My jaw clenched and my eyes narrowed. The very idea had me furious and livid. "Don't even think about it, sweetheart." This time the endearment was laced with a little warning.

She held up one hand. "It was just an example. Now you know how I feel about you going in a place like that. The women there, they expect...things."

"They do. I told you last night, I'm only going to be giving those...things to you."

She shook her head. "It doesn't matter. What happens if they force you?"

I laughed, rich and loud. "Force me?"

She pursed her lips and realized her question was a tad ridiculous.

"I do not like it," she said simply.

That statement gave me pause, for it had more weight than anything else she'd said. "I want to bring the woman to justice, Piper. I want to bring closure to the entire case, to let those who were murdered rest in peace. Hey," I said, getting her to look at me. "Your possessiveness is very appealing. I like that it bothers you."

She frowned. "I should just go in there for you."

I pulled on the reins of my horse and stopped. She had to turn around so we could continue our conversation, this time facing each other. "What the hell do you mean by that?"

"You're a man. A bounty hunter. What woman is going to give information to you?"

"A woman who wants money."

She shook her head. "If Miss Carter is there, she's not going to just *let* you take her. If you go around and ask questions she'll get suspicious, or even learn you're there to arrest her and flee."

"I can handle one woman," I countered. Her words had my manliness in jeopardy. Besides, my ire at Miss Carter was enough where I could certainly handle her.

"It would be easier if I did it for you."

"How?" I had an idea of what she was going to say, but I wanted to be sure before I made conclusions.

"I will go in seeking a job as a prostitute."

I laughed, but this time her words weren't overly humorous. "You just fucked for the first time last night. I don't think you'll be mistaken for a whore."

She shook her head. "Doesn't matter. I can easily play a woman fallen on hard times. A virgin, or almost virgin. I should fetch a fair price."

I didn't want to think about the men circling around her eager to get their hands, and other parts of their anatomy, on her.

"No."

I spurred my horse into movement.

"Why not?" she called from behind me.

"Because I'm your husband, and I forbid it." I wasn't thinking logically. If it were anyone else, the plan had merit, but I couldn't let Piper into a place like that, with men like that, expecting her to fuck or do other dark things. No way in fucking hell.

"You thought I was guilty of murder just the other day and now you're protecting me?" She trotted her horse up next to mine.

"You were innocent of the crime and I'm protecting you because you're my wife. You're *mine.* When you showed up in Ethel's room last night you chose to be mine. I didn't make you. It was your decision. You grabbed my cock, sweetheart."

There was no question who she belonged to and she was *not* going to go to that brothel. No way in hell.

PIPER

I WAS NOT GOING to let Wiley go into another brothel. The temptation of the other women was too great. Did he get a good look at Ethel? She had breasts and hips and lips and was so pretty and certainly knew more about fucking than I did in my little finger. I couldn't compete with her in any way. Why Wiley had chosen me over her was obvious. I'd had my hand on his cock and I was free. I was his wife and he could use and fuck me any way he wished. It sounded harsh, but it was true. He was so handsome, so...virile, that he could have any woman he wanted. He hadn't *wanted* to marry me, so why should he change his ways?

He'd said he didn't want another, but it was hard to believe him. It was hard to believe any man, especially after the way my family had betrayed me, lied to me and used me. If my own family treated me that way, then Wiley was certainly going to as well. He'd end up with another woman at some point, but he wasn't going to do it when I knew about it, when I could do something about it.

We rode into Carey as the sun was setting. It was smaller than Banning so it wouldn't be hard to find the local brothel. I feigned a headache and Wiley had been gentlemanly enough to secure us a room at the hotel before taking the horses to the livery. Once he rode off in that direction to have the animals tended for the night, I ducked out and worked my way to the brothel. It was much more obvious to me now than when in Banning, for it seemed they were all the same. Slipping in through the back door, I was greeted with a similar arrangement than the night before. Two women were eating at the table dressed solely in their undergarments. An older woman was cooking at the stove, the scent of baked bread and stew filling the warm kitchen.

All three women looked me over. While I swallowed down my fear and nerves, I was fortunate to have experience to know what to expect. I assumed a little naiveté only helped my act. While I knew Wiley would miss me when he returned, hopefully I could get some information out of some of these ladies like I had the night before, and then slip out.

"Hello, I wanted to ask...I mean, do you think I could—"

"Lookin' for a job, honey?" the cook asked. The same question was asked by the ladies in Banning. It seemed women came to the back door for work with such frequency they expected it. "If not, you get yourself right on home now."

She waved a spoon at me but I did not retreat. I held my ground. This wasn't as easy this time. I couldn't just ask her after Miss Carter, for all I knew one of these women could be Miss Carter and she was supposedly quite dangerous. While I doubted she kept a gun in her corset or drawers, it didn't mean she wasn't deadly. I could leave and let Wiley do his job, but I didn't want him anywhere near the likes of these women. But then I thought of my husband and remembered how he'd spanked me when I'd just shown up in a brothel, not getting a *job* in one. I didn't have to worry about Miss Carter doing it; he'd kill me himself

"Well?"

I swallowed and shook my head. "No. No thank you," I replied before fleeing out the door.

I all but ran back to the hotel and up the steps. When I pushed open the door to our room, Wiley stopped his pacing and turned to me. "Where the hell have you been?" His voice boomed in the small space.

"I couldn't do it," I replied, trying to catch my breath. My hand was against my chest and I felt my heart pounding.

He narrowed his eyes. "Do what? Leave me?"

"What? No. Why would I do that?"

He shook his head and repeated, "Where the hell have you been?"

"I wanted to find out about Miss Carter so you didn't have to go to another brothel."

He approached me and put his hands on my upper arms. His hold was firm, his touch warm. "What...did...you...do?"

I swallowed. "I...I went to the back door of the brothel."

"After I distinctly told you not to?"

"You were going to go there after I distinctly told you I didn't like it," I countered.

"It's my job!" he replied.

"I'm your wife!" I shouted.

Before I could even realize his intentions, his mouth was on mine and I was pressed up against the door. I felt hard wood at my back and solid muscle and hard male at my front. His tongue plundered and tangled with mine, his big hands gripping my arms. It was all heat and energy, the kiss. I didn't need to breathe when I had Wiley kissing me. I could live off his kiss.

He kissed along my jaw to my ear, nipping at the lobe, then kissing the soft spot beneath it.

"Wiley, I...I need—"

He kissed along the length of my neck and whispered, "What do you need, sweetheart, besides a stern spanking?"

What did I need? "I need...I need you to want *me*. I need you to take me because you ache for me just as much as I ache for you, not just because I'm your wife. I need you to—"

His brow went up as his hand wrapped around my nape to hold me in place. "Need me to what?"

"Take *me*."

His eyes narrowed, but the green darkened, his jaw clenched. "You want me to fuck you, sweetheart?"

I nodded.

"I should spank your ass red, but I'm going to fuck you instead. I can't be gentle this time."

I shook my head. "No. No, I don't want you to be gentle. I want to get lost in you."

I didn't say more. I didn't need to. Wiley lowered

his head and kissed me. It wasn't gentle, but an all-out assault. His mouth ravaged mine, his tongue plundering. Just kissing him was wild and decadent and my body instantly responded. My nipples pebbled beneath my corset and my thighs grew slick with my arousal. In less than a day, my body had recognized Wiley's mastery and willingly submitted.

I wanted what only he could give me and I wanted it now.

"Wiley, please," I begged against his lips.

He lifted his head and brought his hands to the front of my dress. Gripping both sides of the bodice, he ripped it open, off my shoulders and down my arms so they were trapped by my sides. Now I knew what he meant about not being so careful. It was...exhilarating! I could do nothing as he worked the stays of my corset free until the sides opened and my breasts spilled free. He kicked the door shut then pushed me against it, my back pressed into the hard wood. Lowering his head, he took one nipple into his mouth. Instead of the sweet, gentle exploration he'd done earlier, this was...oh. He sucked and licked and tugged at it while his hand worked my other breast. His fingers plucked and tugged at the nipple just shy of being painful. I cried out and winced. The sharpness of his actions morphed into heat and I felt my inner walls clenching.

Somehow my nipples were in direct connection with my woman's core and it wanted to be filled, for I felt empty without Wiley's cock within. He didn't stop his ardent attentions on my breasts, not until my knees became weak and I began to slump. He reached down and pulled up the long hem of my dress, pushing it up and securing it by wrapping his arm about my waist. With his free hand, he yanked at my drawers and they tore and fell to the floor.

"Take my cock out," he breathed.

I hastily worked at the placket of his pants, tugging and fighting with the material until his cock sprang free. It was a dark, ruddy red, a pulsing vein running up the thick length. The wide head had clear fluid seeping from the tip. I didn't have time to ogle, for Wiley closed the small distance between us and pressed his torso into mine. Hooking one of my knees with his hand, he lifted my leg to spread me wide as I felt him nudge against my opening. In one shift of his hips he filled me, trapped as I was between his strong body and the hard door. He didn't go slowly, didn't ease me into being filled so completely. Instead, he pulled back and thrust into me once again.

"Wiley!" I cried out. The sheer intensity of his claiming stole my breath. Wiley did not stop his motions, only began to move faster, deeper. Harder.

I lifted up, wrapping my free leg about his waist that enabled him to shift my hips and go even deeper. How, I didn't know. I just knew that the way he stroked over me, the way his body rubbed against that small place between my thighs that ached and heated had me almost to the brink of my pleasure. I recognized it now, recognized how my pleasure grew and grew, overwhelming me to the point where there was no sight, no sound, only feeling. This time, it was coming upon me so quickly that I didn't have time to do anything but tilt my head back against the door and let go.

"Yes!" I cried. "Oh, it feels so good," I crooned as Wiley's hips pounded me. I was caught upon his cock; there was nothing I could do but let the feelings of being impaled by such a wicked instrument rush over me.

"Good girl, Piper," he breathed. "It's my turn now."

He pushed deep, held still as he groaned. I felt his seed scalding hot within my depths, filling me to overflowing. This was what I'd needed. I'd needed him taking me without measure, using me, yet forcing me to succumb to the pleasure only Wiley could find within me.

Slowly, Wiley lowered my legs to the ground, yet held me in place. The lower part of my dress slipped back down over my legs. I felt his seed trickle out, drip down my thighs and most likely onto the floor at my feet. My arms were still pinned to my sides, my breasts exposed. I saw that my nipples were tightly furled and a bright cherry red. Wiley had not been gentle.

"Are you all right?" he asked, adjusting himself back into his pants, buttoning the placket. He watched me carefully. "I wasn't too rough?"

"Too rough?" I laughed. "That was...incredible."

He looked me over as he grinned. This was the

smile of a well-satisfied man. "I like to see you this way as if I've just captured you and had my way."

"You did," I countered.

"Mmm," he replied noncommittally. "You seem to enjoy a little rough play."

"If that was rough play, then yes."

"Good to know." Instead of pulling the dress back up over my shoulders, he tugged it down and off my body. "It appears this dress is no longer serviceable. Neither are your drawers."

With my hands free, my corset also fell to the floor. I was naked except for my boots and thigh length stockings.

"Thank you, Wiley."

"For fucking you?" His gaze raked over my body. "I assure you, no thanks is needed."

I shook my head. "For taking me as you would one of those women."

He didn't look happy by my answer. "Piper, listen to me. I took you that way because I want you. You, Piper Easton. Not some whore. You are my wife, don't you understand that?"

I swallowed the tears that clogged my throat. "But you didn't want to marry me. My family *killed* your father."

"Do I seem uninterested? Unaffected?" His dark eyes bored into me.

I shook my head. "No, but how do I know you won't

leave me for a woman like Ethel? My brother was infatuated with Miss Carter enough to die for her."

He hooked a hand behind my neck and gently pulled me into his chest. "I'm not your brothers or your father. I don't intend to use you."

"But you thought I had left you."

He ran a hand through his hair, making it stand up in places. "My mother left us when I was small. A traveling preacher. I have a very jaded view on women. Now that I know a woman was among the band of criminals that killed my father, an innocent on a train, it is skewed even more."

"So I'm supposed to trust you not to be like my family when you think I'm just like your mother?"

That gave him pause.

"I take my vows to you seriously. I know you're taking our vows seriously as well."

I looked at him, confused.

"Piper, you went to a brothel, again, against my wishes because you are one possessive woman. If you didn't care about me, about our marriage, you wouldn't have done it."

I opened my mouth to speak, but closed it. He was right, which meant I would fight for him all the more.

WILEY

"THERE'S BEEN ANOTHER ROBBERY."

I sat down at the table across from Piper. We were in the hotel restaurant having breakfast and the news of the latest stage robbery was spreading through the room like wildfire.

She put down her coffee cup and leaned toward me. "Was it...her?"

I had that angry, tense feeling I always had when I was on the search for a criminal and couldn't find them in time before they committed another crime. It was frustrating and a little helpless and I hated that. We were getting closer to finding the woman, but now that there had been another robbery, I knew it wasn't just Miss Carter who needed to be caught. One woman couldn't hold up a stage on her own.

"It appears so, but she had help. It was just outside of town yesterday."

"Was anyone hurt?"

I shook my head. "Not this time."

"Then we must act in haste." Her words were so vehement, so strong.

"We?" I asked.

"You went to the brothel last night...after, well after. I don't think you can go snooping around again without raising suspicion."

I cut off a piece of steak and swiped it through my egg. "What are you suggesting?"

She scooted her chair closer to the table and leaned forward even more so she could speak so only I could hear. If she leaned forward any more her breasts would be in her breakfast plate.

"I will go in once again looking for a job." She glanced left and right to ensure no one overheard. "My nerves got the best of me last night and returning will only show I'm eager but fearful. It will be much more realistic."

"Realistic?" The idea of Piper becoming a whore, even just pretending to do so, made my food taste like sawdust. I put my fork down on my plate. "Realistic would be for you to stay out of this like a good girl."

"Do you just live like this, going from town to town searching for bad people?" she asked, eyeing me speculatively. "Is this what our marriage is going to be, hotels and hunting?"

I frowned. "No, of course not. I have a ranch, The Crossings. It's a few days ride from here. It was my plan to capture the men who did the robberies, killed those people from the train, take the reward money and be a rancher. It was my last job. *This* is to be my last job, finding Miss Carter."

She smiled. "I think I will enjoy being the wife of a rancher."

For some reason, the pleasure on her face, the satisfied tone of her voice settled something inside me. She wanted to go to The Crossings, wanted to live as a rancher's wife. She wanted what I wanted. Then she continued to speak and ruined it.

"The sooner we find this woman, the sooner you

can leave the life of a bounty hunter behind. If I can already be in the brothel, you can choose me and we can search for her together."

While her idea had merit, I didn't like the idea of her being in a place such as that, with the off chance she might have to...service someone else, let alone being near a woman and potentially others, who were dangerous enough to rob stages and kill people.

"You're going to what, go to the back door, get this job and then deflect men's advances until I arrive?"

She nodded. "Yes!"

I leaned forward so our noses practically touched. "If I don't agree to this, you're going to show up there anyway, aren't you?"

"Do you have a choice?"

I leaned back in my chair and crossed my ankles. "Hell, yes. I can take you upstairs and tie you to the bed to keep you right where I want you. Safe and sound and naked."

Her eyes flared with desire at my words.

"We have all day, sweetheart, before the brothel opens for business. Whatever shall we do?"

She looked down at the table and I enjoyed seeing her innocence, pleased to know I hadn't taken it completely by the way I'd taken her. My cock hardened, thankfully hidden beneath the breakfast table. I shifted to a more comfortable position in my chair.

She'd sat a horse after losing her virginity and

being well fucked and then I'd taken her roughly against the door. Surely her pussy needed a break.

"Sore, sweetheart?" I whispered.

She frowned at my question, and then her cheeks flushed. "A...a little," she replied.

"Come." I stood and held out my hand. I could spend the day tending to my wife. I ordered a bath as we walked past the front desk and once the tub and hot water was delivered, I undressed Piper myself and helped her into the steaming water. I didn't hesitate, but slipped a finger over her tender folds to assess how sore *a little* really was.

She winced slightly.

"Poor baby. The hot water will soothe all your aches away."

As I washed her hair, she sighed. "Why are you doing this? I thought you would spend the day arguing with me about my idea."

My hands paused in her soapy tresses. I *could* do that. I wanted to rail against the plan, but it had some merit. She didn't need to know that and while I had her naked in a tub, her nipples just above the surface of the hot water, I wasn't going to talk about it. "I'm tending to my wife," I said simply.

A smile tipped up the corner of her mouth. "You tended to me quite effectively last night."

"Mmm," I replied. "And I will tend to you again later."

"Really? I did not realize it could be done so often."

I took a glass and filled it with water from the tub. "Tilt your head back." I rinsed the soap from her hair as I spoke. "As many times as we want. When this is all over and we get to The Crossings, I may not let you out of bed for a week."

"A week? What can we do in a week? Haven't we done it all the possible ways?"

I rinsed her hair, and then refilled the glass. "You've learned only two of the ways so far."

"You mean gentle one time and rough another."

"Yes," I agreed. "Also, one time you were on your back, the next up against a wall. There are many ways to fuck, many levels of intensity."

"Will you show them all to me?"

"Show them?" I put the glass down. "We'll do them all. Together."

I didn't let Piper leave the room until it was the sun had set; I even had our meals delivered to us instead of making our way to the restaurant. There was nothing outside the four walls of the room that I desired, my focus being solely on my new wife. I knew that keeping the door closed kept all of our marital challenges at bay for having her beneath me, above me, all around me we were in complete accord.

I had not wanted a wife but had been forced to wed. Piper was married to the man who'd killed one of her brothers and brought her family to justice. She, too, had married under duress. But instead of considering these things, I'd taken her to bed and showed her ways to fuck while allowing her sore pussy to heal. While my cock certainly liked being deep inside her, it had been assuaged by a myriad other carnal activities.

When she stirred from a nap after I'd made her come by my tongue and gentle fingers, I agreed to her plan.

"You may go to the brothel." The words came out bitter and with much effort.

She sat up in bed so surprised she forgot to cover herself with the sheet. I groaned at the sight of her pert breasts.

"I have rules, however."

She nodded her head in agreement. I assumed she would agree to anything I had to say at the moment considering.

"You may not go into a room alone with any man but me. I don't care if you run out of there screaming."

"Yes, Wiley."

"You will not flaunt yourself at any time, to anyone."

"Flaunt myself?" she placed her hand on my chest and swirled her finger through the smattering of hair. I stilled her hand.

"You will see. Lastly, and most importantly, when I claim you, you will do whatever I say, do you understand?"

"Yes, Wiley."

I didn't like this, but I didn't have much choice. If I wanted to capture not only Miss Carter, but also her new cohorts in crime, I needed Piper's help. She could assist me in ways another man could not. I doubted anyone would imagine a woman infiltrating a brothel to capture a criminal had ever been done before. If Piper wasn't my wife, I'd have to consider this tactic to be smart.

Instead, I gritted my teeth the entire way to the brothel. We walked in silence in the warm night until we stopped just down the block. I pulled her in for a kiss before releasing her. She was warm and pliant and her scent swirled around us.

I should just skip finding Miss Carter and whisk Piper back to the ranch, leave all the danger behind. I loosened my grip and let her go. It was one of the hardest things I'd ever had to do and as I watched her slip in through the back door, I knew I'd have to ensure her safety.

Walking around to the front of the establishment, I went in and ordered a whiskey, then waited. I'd be the first to claim her; there was no question.

6

IPER

THIS WAS the third time I walked in the backdoor of a brothel. It was getting easier each time, perhaps because I knew that Wiley was around...somewhere to protect me. Perhaps it was because I was much more bold and daring than I'd ever been in my life. I'd been so sheltered on the ranch. Even with my family off doing terrible crimes, I had remained unaware and safe. Now, I was very aware and possibly not safe. I had to do this for Wiley, to let him have the revenge he deserved and the closure he so desperately sought. Only then could we get on with our lives, settle into his ranch and just...be.

The cook stood in the same place before the stove

and looked at me, again with no expression or surprise. "Back, are you?"

I nodded, "Yes, ma'am. I'm...I'm desperate."

She looked me over in an assessing way again, then nodded.

She went to a swinging door, pushed it open. "Regina!"

A moment later, a small woman with brown hair came into the room. She wore a corset so snug her breasts practically touched her chin. She had gaudy red lips and black kohl lined her eyes. "Got a new one for you. It'll be a busy night, so Sheila's too busy to talk to you now."

Sheila. My heart leapt at the sound of her name.

"You'll get a dollar a lay, an extra dollar for anything beyond a pussy fuck. You make that clear up front. Have any questions, Regina will help you tonight. Come sunrise, we'll get you all squared away."

She looked me over. "Have you eaten?"

"Yes, ma'am," I said again.

"Good. Regina, get her something to wear and get her out on the floor. You ever fucked before?"

The woman was brash and crude, but she was going to have me ready for my first customer quickly enough. She didn't seem like one to dawdle.

I felt my cheeks heat, but nodded.

"Not much, I would guess, and the men will see that. By the end of the night I'd guess you'll be innocent no longer."

She turned back to the stove and Regina led me upstairs. It was only when the woman held up a corset with frilly edges did the full impact of my situation settle upon me. I had to hope that Wiley was below.

An hour later, I walked into what I assumed was a parlor with Regina. While she'd been nice and helped me dress, she'd been fairly quiet. I hadn't wanted to press her with questions about Miss Carter for fear that she would think something amiss, but I just asked after if her employer was fair. She nodded her head but kept her lips pinched closed. Perhaps the silence was telling in itself.

As I entered the room, I felt exposed. If I tugged on the top of my corset, the petticoat would only ride higher up my legs. If I tugged the petticoat down, I was sure my breasts would pop free. There was nothing I could do but tolerate the indecency of the outfit. I thought of the night I was forced to wear just the sheet and it eased my concerns a bit. Of course, the result of that night was a hasty wedding. I could not fathom what this night would bring. As several men had their eyes, very keen and interested eyes, on me, I could now clearly see Wiley's concern. It was one thing for him to come into a brothel and talk with a woman. He could feign disinterest and leave. I, on the other hand, could not.

A tall, thin man with a mustache approached but was cut off by Wiley. I exhaled a pent up breath and attempted to hide my relief at the sight of him. The others were no comparison; Wiley was the handsomest man in the room. He was also the biggest and with an intent expression on his face unlike the others. He would have me and I could feel my pussy getting wet at the thought.

"Hello. Do you like peppermint?" he asked.

"I beg your pardon?" I asked, frowning. I had not expected such an odd question.

"Hello, there. I'm Ruby. Aren't you a brawny one?" a woman said, wrapping her arm around Wiley's thick biceps.

I tried to keep a bland expression, but it was hard.

Ruby tilted her head in my direction. "She's new. Look at her, she's so new she doesn't know what she's doing."

Wiley made a rumbling sound deep in his chest. "Mmm, I like that. I can show her just what she needs to do."

Put out, Ruby replied, "If you come down a little later lacking satisfaction, you come see me, all right?"

"Yes, ma'am," Wiley replied dutifully.

"Now, where were we? Oh yes. Do you like peppermint?"

I was completely taken aback. "Yes. Yes, I like peppermint."

He pulled a stick from his shirt pocket and handed it to me.

I shook my head. "No, thank you."

"I insist." He held it out to me, his expression blank.

I frowned, but took the preferred treat. "Tonight, I'd like to teach you something."

Wiley looked around the room and signaled to a burly man by the door. He nodded back and then Wiley escorted me upstairs. "Which room is yours?" he asked. His voice was loud, clear and a complete act.

I pointed down the hall. "This way."

I opened the door and let him precede me in. It was very similar to Ethel's room at the brothel in Banning except this bed was smaller.

Like in the hotel room, Wiley pressed me back against the closed door and began kissing along my neck. As he did so, he whispered. "I'm sure we are being watched. They will want to know of your abilities and whether to keep you."

I stiffened in his hold. Where would people be to observe us? I couldn't look around and search and give ourselves away.

"No, don't lose that stiff backbone now, sweetheart."

I angled my head to the side so he could have better access.

"I won't fuck you with an audience, and besides, you're too sore, but we'll have to give everyone a show. Will that make you hot, being watched?"

I moaned at the idea. Knowing Wiley was here to take care of me, I had to let go, to let him do his job.

I turned my head so I could kiss along his neck this time, my hands tangling in his hair. "Yes," I replied, my voice breathy. Anyone who was observing would think

I liked his attentions, which was completely true. "A woman named Sheila runs the establishment."

"Good. I'll track her down. Later. First though, trust me, sweetheart," he murmured, before he stepped back. My skin was overheated and my nipples were tight.

"Where's that peppermint stick?" he asked.

I held it in my hand, forgotten.

"Suck it."

The candy's flavor was like sweet ice against my tongue. I'd had a peppermint stick before from the mercantile owner in Zenith, but that had been years earlier. It made my mouth water and my lips and tongue tingle.

Wiley sat down on the edge of the bed, toed off his shoes and began taking off his shirt as he spoke. "What's your name, sweetheart?"

"Piper," I replied.

"Well, Piper, how much is good cock suck?"

His crude words had me pausing, then I pushed away from the wall. "Oh, um. A dollar."

He pulled a coin from his pants and slapped it onto the table beside the bed.

"Are you a virgin?" he asked.

He knew the answer, but I knew this was all for show so I played along.

"No."

"But you're new."

"Yes."

"Ever had your pussy eaten out?"

I flushed at the image in my mind; Wiley's head between my thighs, his large hands holding me still as his thumbs parted my pussy lips and he licked me. Everywhere. He even nibbled and sucked on the bundle of nerves he called my clit. I heated all over just thinking about the pleasure he'd wrought from my body with just his tongue. I nodded.

"Ever sucked a cock before?"

"No," I replied.

"Good. I like knowing I'll be your first. I'm going to teach you how to suck my cock." He shucked his shirt to the floor and opened the front of his pants. "Pretend the candy's my cock. You're doing an excellent job at sucking on it. Take it out of your mouth and lick around the top. Good, like that."

He grasped his erect cock at the base in his fist, sliding it up and down in a slow motion. Clearly he had no concern about being observed. I decided I would forget about anyone else and concentrate solely on Wiley. It wasn't a hard task, for the sight mesmerized me, the way he worked himself and knowing what felt good, but my inner walls clenched down in anticipation of being filled by such a beast. I wanted him to fuck me, but not here. Not now.

"See how I'm running my fist up and down the base, take the candy into your mouth so it touches the back of your throat, then back out."

I did as he said, almost transfixed by his words.

"The candy is much narrower than my cock, but it will give you an idea of what it feels like to have something nudge that far in your mouth."

When the hard stick touched the back of my throat, my eyes watered and I coughed, quickly pulling the candy out. "I...I can't," I sputtered.

"Shh," he crooned. "Take it in not quite as far. See how far you can go before you have to pull back. You're such a good girl, I could come just watching you."

I set a rhythm, learning how deep I could take the candy into my mouth before I instinctively wanted to expel it. I did it over and over, the tingly sweet taste coating my tongue.

"Good, now set the stick down and get on your knees." He spread his knees wider making room for me. When I settled between his legs his cock was only inches from my mouth. The broad head was plum colored and fluid seeped from the tip.

"Lick it off, sweetheart."

I did, the taste of him merging with the flavor of the candy.

"Now lick around the head and take me deep. Just like that stick."

Flicking my tongue out, I circled the flared head, then opened wide so it could fit into my mouth. His skin was hot, yet soft against my tongue. Hard, yet velvety in texture. Taking him deeper, he filled me up, my mouth stretched unbelievably wide.

"The peppermint tingles my skin," he hissed as I

felt his palm caress my head, his fingers tangling in my hair. With his hand still around the base, I began to move so he went in and out of my mouth, just as he'd directed with the candy. The treat had been hard and cool against my tongue but Wiley's cock warmed me and pulsed and grew within my mouth. I picked up his clean scent, the taste of him salty and sweet.

He reached and tugged down the front of my corset so my breasts sprang free. His hands raked over the nipples until they tightened. I moaned around his cock at the feel of his hands on me, but I didn't stop.

"You're so good at this, Piper. I'm going to come. You're making me come."

I felt him thicken as he groaned, his body tense and rigid as I felt pulse after pulse of his seed against my tongue, coating it. The hand in my hair tightened until finally, his emissions ceased and he pulled me off of him.

I tilted my chin up to see if he was pleased.

"Swallow, sweetheart." He stroked my chin with his thumb and I did just that, taking his seed into my body just as he would if he filled my pussy. The flushed cheeks and sated gleam in his eye, made me feel powerful. I'd done this to him and I reveled in it. Knowing I could reduce such a strong man to his basest of instincts was heady and very arousing. I squirmed where I knelt, feeling the wetness his pleasure had brought about.

Wiley exhaled loudly, then grinned. "Your turn, sweetheart."

"But...but you only paid for me to suck your cock."

There, I'd said the bold words, remembering our act, although my arousal was not pretend.

He picked me up from beneath my arms and tossed me onto the bed as if I weighed nothing. "I'm a gentleman when it comes to fucking. You might be a whore, but you have needs, don't you?"

"Oh yes," I sighed. I had needs and I wanted him to meet them so badly.

"You are wearing far too many clothes." He undid the ribbon of my petticoat and it fell to the floor. I stood before him naked except for a corset with my breasts exposed above the lacy edge. Wiley still remained in just his pants, but his cock thrust from the opening as if he hadn't just come.

"What do you plan to do?" I asked. The wicked gleam in his eye had me curious, not fearful. He might be dangerous or even hard in his role as bounty hunter, but as a husband, he was very attentive and extremely thorough. As a customer in a brothel, he was very hot.

He crawled up onto the bed with me like a predator hunting its prey. "I paid for a cock suck, but that doesn't mean I can't play. I've taken your mouth. Has anyone taken your ass?"

I frowned, confused. "I...I don't understand."

"Oh good. You have a virgin ass."

"Virgin ass?" I squeaked. "That will, I mean, I'm sure I should charge more money."

"I'm just going to play tonight. I'll have to come back and play some more. Would you like that?"

I looked up into his dark eyes and nodded.

"Then save that ass for me, for my cock, all right?" He pulled out another coin and placed it on the table. "There. Now I want to play." Wiley positioned himself between my legs, spreading them wide, then sliding his fingers up the insides of my thighs so that he touched my pussy, running over my slick folds. "So wet, sweetheart."

His voice sounded almost reverent, as if the state of my arousal was an indication on the status of our marriage. Perhaps it was, for I was quite pleased with my husband at the moment, especially when he slipped one finger very slightly into my pussy, only far enough to run over that specific spot that had me dripping and writhing for him. But when he slipped his other hand lower and touched my back entrance, my perspective changed entirely.

"You can't mean—"

"Oh yes. I'm not going to take you there tonight, for I'm too big and you are much too tight. For now though, I'll just play—and make you come. Remember, I paid to fuck this ass first."

His finger brushed ever so lightly over that forbidden spot and I imagined him to possibly be correct, for the feelings just the slightest touch of his finger elicited heated my skin and softened all of my limbs. It was intense and decadent and dark.

"Is this something people really do?" I asked, unclear about this illicit act.

"Oh yes. And as my little whore, you're going to love it."

He seemed so confident, so sure that what he was doing would be something I found pleasurable. Based on the brief touch of his finger, it was possible I might, but having his entire digit deep within me sounded painful. And his cock? I had no concept of how he would fit. It was so snug when he fucked my pussy, but my back entrance? I was doubtful.

"Take a deep breath, sweetheart. Relax."

"It's hard to relax when you have a finger that wants into your ass," I grumbled.

He paused, tossed his head back and laughed, rich and deep. "Oh, a whore who has a sense of humor. Don't taunt me, sweetheart, for most men would take you now, whether you were prepared or not. I like my woman willing and pliant."

Another chink of that wall broke and my willpower to fight him in this most unusual of attentions ceased. I sighed into the quilt and let all of my muscles relax. I had to trust that he would take care of me, especially in this most unusual of places.

As soon as I gave up all resistance, his finger pushed past the ring of muscle that had been resisting his entry to fill me to the first knuckle. I groaned; I couldn't help the almost feral sound that escaped my lips. The sensation was unlike anything I'd ever felt before, anything Wiley had wrought from my body. It was jangly and intense and...odd, but while the stretching burned slightly, the feel was unlike anything I'd ever imagined. The combination of his fingers in both of my holes was too much, too powerful, too *intense.* I came, my entire body tightening like a bow, my inner walls clenching down on both of his digits. It seemed, all of a sudden, that just the very tips of his fingers weren't enough. My body wanted more, wanted to be filled completely, not just my pussy but my ass as well.

"Good girl," he said. "You are so beautiful when you come. Your nipples are pink little tips that I want to suck. Your ass is so tight it's all but strangling my finger. I'll come back and fuck this ass and you're going to love it. I promise. You're still coming? Such a good little whore."

His words continued, some offering praise, some vowing further carnal delights. Words such as *whore,* reminding me that we were in a brothel. We were play-acting, but only a little, for I wasn't faking anything and I had a feeling neither was Wiley.

WILEY

"Sweetheart, you were better than I was expecting. I think I need to find out how much you cost for the night." I pulled on my clothes, ready to go and find Miss Carter. If she really did run the establishment, then she'd be the one collecting the money.

Piper tugged at the blanket to cover herself as she watched me. "All night?"

I looked at her over my shoulder and grinned. She had the well-fucked look about her and I couldn't help but feel powerful knowing I made her look that way. "Seems you're more of a virgin than I thought. I think it'll be fun to leave my mark in more than one place. Get dressed," I added.

She frowned. "I thought you just said you wanted me for the night."

"I'm not leaving you here all alone, sweetheart. Some other man might lay claim and I'm not done with you."

It was clear my meaning, for she gave up on her modesty in exchange for leaving. It took longer for her to dress and I became impatient, not even letting her finish the buttons up the front of her dress before I tugged her out into the hall.

At the top of the stairs a whore was leading a man by the hand, most likely toward her room.

"Where can I find the owner?"

She frowned, but pointed. "Down the stairs and her office is toward the back."

I didn't delay, just grasped Piper's hand in mine and

made my way there. Glancing down at Piper, I offered her a small smile as I squeezed her hand in reassurance before I knocked on the door.

A woman called for us to enter.

She was older than I thought, perhaps in her thirties, definitely older than Kevin Sinclair. If she'd been involved in the recent stage robbery, then she'd enlisted new men to help her, clearly using her charms to do so, and she wasn't lacking in them. She was actually quite beautiful. She had blond hair in perfect ringlets artfully styled. Her dress was a pale blue silk with a bright sheen to it. Her breasts were ample and on full display above the low cut of her bodice. In the past I might have even taken a tumble upstairs with her.

"I'm interested in paying for this little lady for the night."

"She's a good cock sucker then?" Her perfectly curved brow arched. She had been watching.

"Very. But it sounds as if you already know that."

She turned to her desk, opened a drawer and turned back, a gun in hand.

"Yes, Mr. Easton. I know many things."

I felt Piper's tight grip on my arm as I shoved her behind me.

"Miss Carter, I presume?"

She offered a tight smile, which was all the confirmation I needed.

I felt like we were in a showdown, for this was a

fight I had to win. She'd killed my father and robbed several stages and a train. She hadn't done it alone, but she was guilty. I wanted justice for my father and having her behind bars, or even swinging by a rope around her neck, would do it nicely. It would be sweet justice to see her dead.

"I heard there was a bounty hunter in town and it is quite the coincidence you took such a fancy to my new girl. Your use of your employees is quite ingenious, especially one related to Kevin Sinclair. Piper's such an unusual name. You should remember whores don't use their real names."

"You can't get out of here," I told her.

She looked at me in mock horror, and then laughed. "Oh really? I believe I'm the one holding the gun."

The door opened and the man from the parlor entered. He was clearly the muscle of the place for his he was built like a whiskey barrel and had no neck. A scar ran down his left cheek and I doubted he knew how to smile.

"Kill him, but not here," she told the man.

"No!" Piper shouted pulling me back away from the man. She was not helping one bit. The man approached but I fought him. It was hard to block his punches with Piper behind me.

"You, you're coming with me. The Sinclairs have been useful in the past and I have no doubt you'll be even more...motivated than your brother." Miss Carter shifted her weapon to aim at Piper. What she planned for her wasn't mentioned, but I could only imagine. Kevin Sinclair, like most men, were led around by their dick, which made them only so helpful to a woman like Miss Carter. Piper, on the other hand, wouldn't offer such challenges and would be easier to handle. I was distracted by the gun, and using my body to shield her as best I could, when the man caught me with a wild punch.

"Wiley!" I heard before the world went black.

PIPER

"He's going to find me," I vowed as I stumbled into a pitch-black space, hitting the far wall without my hands to stop me. My wrists were bound before me, the blood long gone from my fingers. I flexed them but they were numb, as the binding was too snug for comfort. Miss Carter was silhouetted in the dim light of the doorway. We'd ridden half the night to some ranch or homestead, the direction unclear. I did know that I was alone with no one to know where I was.

"No, he won't. He's dead. Arthur always takes care of it. Having the bounty hunter unconscious makes it even easier."

The word *always* was not missed. How many times

had they done this before? Her confidence had mine faltering. Was Wiley dead? Arthur was a big man, much bigger even than Wiley and no doubt had the skill and lack of conscience to see it done.

"Rest. You're going to need it," she replied, slamming the door shut. I heard the metal of a lock sliding into place securing me in this pitch-black room. The floor was wood beneath my feet but there were no windows, nothing to let in light except for a tiny seam beneath the door. I lowered myself to the floor and leaned against the wall. I was exhausted, not only physically but mentally as well. I thought of Wiley and what was happening to him, nothing else was important. What the woman intended for me was also unknown to me, but I was still alive. She considered me useful, somehow, which gave me hope that an opportunity to escape would arise.

Nothing would happen now. If I was weary, so was Miss Carter. Nothing would happen before the sun rose and there was nothing I could do to help Wiley at the moment either. I lay down on the hard wood, my knees tucked up as I stared at the sliver of dim light. The air was still, but cool, and I shivered, remembering the feel of Wiley's chest as my pillow, his warmth, the sound of his heart beating against my ear. A tear slipped down my cheek at the realization that the man I'd hated was really the man I loved. Danger and imminent death brought out true emotion, made one realize many things, stripping away the heated emotions and displayed the unvarnished truth. I closed my eyes and pictured his wicked grin, the intensity in his eyes just before he kissed me, the abandoned look on his face as he came. I fell asleep to this, hoping beyond all hopes that they would not just be a memory, but that I would get to see the real thing again soon.

WILEY

Miss Carter's henchman was no challenge for me once I realized Miss Carter had taken Piper. The man didn't stand a chance as he drove a wagon out into the prairie. He'd dumped me in the back while I was still unconscious but had only bound my wrists. Perhaps he was a cocky bastard and didn't think I'd put up much of a fight, or maybe he'd hit his other victims—surely there were others—much harder. I had motivation and love on my side and the man's brawn was no match.

With her family most likely dead now, Piper had no one. I had no one. No family, besides each other and I couldn't allow her to fend for herself. Miss Carter was cunning and could easily use another woman to use in her criminal activity. This and this alone reassured me that Piper would remain alive and whole for at least the short term. When her usefulness ended, so would her life.

I hadn't wanted a bride, but I'd gotten one. Piper most certainly hadn't wanted the man who'd hauled her to jail for a groom, but I'd claimed her. I hadn't known what love was, but discovered it readily enough. I imagined Piper felt the same, but neither of us had said the words. There had been no time, or perhaps I just hadn't realized it until now, until the dire realization that I could lose her. I didn't know Miss Carter's plans, but this bastard was going to tell me. And when he was beneath me on the hard ground beside the wagon and as I held his gun to his head, he did.

7

IPER

I WAS THIRSTY AND STIFF, my body aching from the floor. Sunlight came through the slit in the door and I must have slept, but I had no idea how long. I was clearly in an ice house, although it was not in use. I remembered the few steps I'd taken before being shoved into the room and it was still fairly cool in the space, even with the sun up. This knowledge did me no good, for as I tried the door, it held fast. That there was a lock on an ice house only meant others had been kept prisoner there before.

Time passed and I searched for a weapon, but there was nothing. No loose boards, no rocks, nothing.

I sat and waited, thirsty and only my thoughts for company.

I must have dozed off, for the rattling of the lock made me stir. I pushed myself up to standing as the door opened, the sunlight blinding me and I held my bound hands to my eyes. Miss Carter came into the room quickly as if shoved, a second person behind her. When he stepped inside, the sun hit him so that I could see him clearly.

"Wiley!" I cried, dashing to his side and gripping his arm. He looked so good, so angry, so...whole.

In his hands he held a gun, aimed solely on Miss Carter.

"Let's get you out of here, sweetheart."

I nodded and practically ran out into the sunshine, squinting.

Wiley and Miss Carter followed.

"Are you hurt?" he asked, looking me over, running a hand over my hair. It had long since fallen from the pins and hung wild down my back.

I shook my head, but wiggled my hands as best I could. He gave a pointed look at the sour faced Miss Carter as he pulled a knife from a sheath attached to his belt. With deft hands, he cut through the binding and I rubbed at my chafed wrists. Feeling came back painfully, but it didn't matter. Nothing mattered but Wiley being alive.

"Should I kill her?" he asked me, his expression

murderous. If I said yes, he'd have shot her then and there, I had no doubt.

I looked to Miss Carter. She was not as meticulously dressed as the previous night. Her blue dress was now wrinkled, her hair in disarray and her expression much less confident.

"Why did you accept the job to find her?" I prompted.

He narrowed his gaze and the hand holding his gun tightened. "To bring my father's killers to justice."

Miss Carter's eyes widened at this. "I didn't know —" she sputtered.

"You didn't know what?" Wiley growled. "The people you killed were real? That they had families? Friends? Lives? My father was all I had and you took him from me. You took loved ones from others, too."

I remembered Wiley's bitterness toward his mother and could only imagine the bond he shared with his father after her departure. Perhaps he took up the profession of a bounty hunter because he needed to make bad people accountable for their actions. He couldn't punish his mother for all the hurt she'd caused, but helping others receive even a small measure of justice slowly healed, or at least soothed, his own measure of anger.

"Will killing her bring you the revenge you're looking for?" I asked. I went to stand beside him, my hand once again on his arm.

He cocked the gun and Miss Carter's cheeks paled.

She took a step back but there was nowhere for her to go. She couldn't outrun a bullet or a man set on vengeance.

"No, but it would certainly be sweet justice."

I shook my head. "You're better than this. Better than she is, than my family. Take her to town. Let her stand before the judge. Let her pay for the crimes so the other victims will know justice has been served." My words were soft, soothing. "It's over, Wiley. It's over."

For a full minute he just glared at Miss Carter, then he lowered the gun and looked down at me, his eyes full of...love? Hope? "No, sweetheart, it's just beginning."

WILEY

PIPER HAD BEEN RIGHT. Handing Miss Carter off to the sheriff of Carey felt good, felt final. I knew the man would keep a close and vigilant eye on her until the circuit judge came around. She'd get the trial she deserved and the conviction warranted. Everyone in Carey and the rest of the Montana Territory would know those who'd robbed the first set of stage coaches and train had been brought to justice.

As I led Piper to the hotel, she asked, "Will you leave to track down the men who helped Miss Carter with the most recent stage robbery?" I could hear the fear and worry lacing her words.

I stopped on the boardwalk and took her hand. Her eyes lifted to mine. They were so green, with the longest pale lashes. "No. I'm done. As I told you before, it's time to be a rancher now. I've got my spread, I've got my cattle and I've got myself a bride."

She smiled brilliantly and I knew I'd made the right decision. I left the past with the sheriff, handing off not only a prisoner, but my life as a bounty hunter as well.

I started walking again, pulling her along with me. "I'm sick of hotels. This will be the last one we stay in. Tomorrow, we ride for the ranch where I will claim you in my bed. Our bed. Is there anything you want, sweetheart, while we're still in town? I don't plan to come this way again anytime soon."

Piper pulled on my arm and I stopped once again. A tremulous smile formed on her lips. "I...I was wondering something."

"Oh?" I asked, brushing her hair back from her face. I couldn't stop touching her. I needed the contact, craved it.

"There's one thing that only you can do for me. To give me something I've always wanted."

"Really?" I asked, intrigued.

She nodded and bit her lip before speaking. "A baby."

My heart flipped, then settled, as if it had been

upside down my entire life and now, with Piper, it was in the perfect place. The idea of her growing big with my seed—that we'd make a beautiful little girl with wheat colored hair—had me realizing that my entire life was standing before me.

"Perhaps we've already made one," I told her, for I'd taken her readily enough since we wed.

She shrugged and looked up at me through her lashes. "It wouldn't hurt to continue our efforts."

"No, it wouldn't hurt in the least." I grinned. "In fact, it will be quite pleasurable."

I had haste on my side now, tugging her as I practically ran to our hotel.

PIPER

Many things had become clear when I realized how perilously close I'd been to losing Wiley. I knew I'd been wrong, I knew he could take care of not only me, but himself as well, but more importantly that I didn't want to live without him. Perhaps when we first wed I was unhappy, but the man had proved me wrong at every turn. And now, as he shut the hotel room door closed behind us and saw his needy expression—for I knew what Wiley looked like when he was highly aroused—there was nowhere else I wanted to be. I wasn't a Sinclair any longer. I was an Easton. I was Mrs. Wiley Easton and I was proud of it.

I curved my hand around his neck and pulled him down for a kiss. Perhaps this was our *real* first kiss, for we both wanted it. We both meant all the longing and love that we put into it. The judge may have married us days ago, but this kiss made it truly real.

We were no longer in danger and that burden was now gone; Wiley had taken it from me and resolved the problem. He was my protector, my lover, my husband. And as we kissed, our tongues tangling, we were no longer sharing only part of ourselves. We were one, and soon, our bodies would be as well.

Wiley lifted his head. "Are you mine?" His cheeks were flushed, his eyes serious yet narrowed in need, our breaths mingled.

I nodded against the bed. "Yes," I whispered.

He moved away from me to recline on the bed, the frame squeaking beneath his heavy weight. "Then show me. Take off your clothes and show me what's mine."

The picture he painted with his words had my eyes flaring and wetness pooling between my thighs. I turned and faced him. He was reclined and leaning on one elbow, relaxed, yet I knew that he would have me beneath him and his cock buried deep inside of me if he chose. He was in complete control now and I loved it. I loved him, so I did as he bid. I knew that if I pleased him in this, he would most certainly please me as well. Not once or twice, but all day long.

I raised my hands to the top buttons of my dress and saw that his eyes followed. I undid one button and his nostrils flared. I undid another and his lips parted. Another and his fingers clenched in the blanket. It was very heady to see my effect on him, for although I was the one removing my clothes; I was getting a similar show. I felt like a woman on a stage in a very naughty act, but with Wiley as my audience, I felt decadent and wanton.

I also felt powerful, for beneath the front placket of his pants, the thick outline of his cock was blatantly visible. I couldn't help the grin that escaped as I undid the last button. I lifted one hand and undid the tiny button there. I took a step toward him and held out my wrist. Wiley looked at it, took it in his big hand and raised it to his lips. He kissed the tender inside, just where my pulse point was. He undid the button at my other wrist, and then kissed the inside of that one as well. The softness and heat of his lips made my body heat. My blood felt hot and sluggish.

Stepping back, I pushed the bodice of the dress off my shoulders, and then let the material gather about my waist so only my corset covered my torso. Wiley's eyes were riveted to the skin that was exposed as I undid the stays; although I realized that perhaps I could taunt him, let him feel as hot and needy by playing the temptress. My breasts were almost free of the corset when I stopped. The top half of my nipples were exposed and the cleavage the half open corset created was plump, full and very decadent.

Wiley's jaw was clenched tight and his eyes narrowed.

Placing one foot up on the edge of the bed, I lifted the hem of my skirt up over my leg, exposing my boot and my stocking clad calf, then further still to uncover my knee, then the tops of the stocking with the pink bow and then the creamy flesh above.

"Jesus," Wiley muttered, his eyes riveted to my leg.

"Oops," I said, my voice as innocent as I could make it. "I forgot to take off my boots."

I worked one off quickly, and then moved to the ribbon just above my knee. Tugging on it, it came loose, then I slid the white stocking down my leg, exposing my skin to his view, one inch at a time. As I leaned forward to slide it off my foot, my breasts practically spilled from the loose confines of my corset.

"Are you trying to kill me, sweetheart?" He pushed up so he sat directly in front of me. Our faces were so close that I could kiss him if I just leaned forward an inch. His eyes were so green, so clear, and so desperate.

I didn't move from my position, but continued to glance up at him through my lashes. "Whatever do you mean?" I asked sweetly.

"If you are, it's a great way to go. But, Piper, I don't want to make a fool of myself and come in my pants. You're just too damn hot. If you're going to tempt me this way, I want you to suck me off the first time so I can last all day for you."

It was my turn to take a deep breath. "You mean come more than once?"

He nodded. "If you suck me off, I'll be able to pay attention to you and work you hard."

The idea was very appealing and he was the most aroused I'd ever seen him. His control was incredible, for he'd be fucking me right now if it snapped.

"All right," I replied. I switched legs, quickly removed my other boot and stocking, yet this time with more haste than temptation. I placed my hands on his thighs and lowered to my knees between them. Opening his pants, his cock sprang free and right toward my mouth. I was always amazed at the sight of it; so big and thick with the bulging veins and broad head. I licked my lips in anticipation, for I knew what it felt like against my tongue, knew the sounds Wiley made when I took him as deep as I could. His deep groan filled the room as I sucked on it, hollowing out my cheeks as I licked around the ridge of the flared head. Grabbing the base in a tight grip, I took him deep, reassured that my hand would keep him from going in too far. So I set to work. It was my mission to have his hips rising off the bed, to make the sounds from his mouth incoherent and desperate, to have his hands tangle in my hair and guide me to how he liked it. But I knew he wouldn't take long to reach his pleasure, for I felt him swell and lengthen in my mouth and his hand tightened against my scalp.

"So good, sweetheart. I'm going to come so take it all." His hips thrust up and he stiffened, groaning, as I felt his seed coat my tongue. He was salty and tangy and it made me continue to suck and work him until he was spent and his hand dropped to the bed beside him.

I pulled off him, swallowed, and then wiped my mouth with the back of my hand.

"Such a good girl, Piper. You're incredible at that. You had me so worked up with your little strip show that I couldn't wait a moment longer."

He grabbed me beneath my arms and pulled me up just as he was falling backward so I lay on top of him. We kissed, our mouths open, our tongues tangling, our passion great. I could feel his cock against my belly, still hard.

"We have way too much clothing on, sweetheart," he said against my mouth.

I laughed, for he'd had me take off my clothes, but stopped me, now he wanted them off again.

"You think this is amusing?"

I nodded, my hair falling down over my forehead.

"This is going to be very serious fucking." He tried to look stern and serious but I knew it was an act.

"Oh?" I asked.

"Very serious, because it won't just be fucking, but

lovemaking. I love you and I want to show you how much."

I tilted my head and my smile went from humorous to sweet. He said the words I'd longed to hear, that I'd hoped to hear, for I felt the same. "I love you, too, and it's all been lovemaking."

"Even that time when I bent you over the bed?"

I blushed at his words, for it had been quite rough...and delicious. "Even then."

He sat up, easily moving me to stand directly before him and undressed me as he spoke. "Then this time will not be a shock to you then."

My corset fell to the floor and his mouth settled over one nipple.

"Oh?" I asked again, this time on a gasp. His attentions to just one breast had my breath catching. He didn't linger, but lifted his head and worked the dress down and over my hips so it pooled on the floor, my drawers quickly following.

Wiley's hands cupped my bottom, holding me in place so I had to meet his heated gaze.

"I want all of you, Piper." As he spoke, his fingers parted the cheeks of my bottom and one finger brushed over my back entrance. I cried out at the illicit touch. "I'm going to fuck your pussy, then I'm going to claim your ass."

His finger circled and probed the back entrance, but did nothing more, however it sparked intense feelings that only this kind of play could bring about. My thighs were slick with my desire and my nipples were tightly furled. I wanted it, even if my mind was worried. But this was the perfect example of when I needed to trust Wiley explicitly. He'd never done anything to hurt me. Never. He'd saved me. He loved me.

That alone had me saying, "Yes."

His grin warmed me and I smiled back, ceding control in this moment and in my body.

"Then let's get you ready."

"Ready?"

Grabbing me about the waist, he tossed me onto the bed with a bounce.

He stood, his cock erect and exposed, and stripped. I was able to look my fill and he pleased me immensely. I was so attracted to him that I had my thighs clench together and try to ease the ache, but it did not work.

Instead of going slowly, he practically tore at his clothes. He grabbed his bag and pulled something from it, a small glass jar, and placed it on the bedside table.

I frowned at it.

"I picked it up at the mercantile along with the peppermints."

"What is it?"

"It's lubricant that I'll use to ease the passage of my cock into your ass."

Wiley had forethought and purchased something

to aid in taking my ass. He'd been thinking about me, planning for just this moment. He may have only just told me he loved me, but his careful consideration and very heated direction of thought had me realizing how much I'd meant to him so early after we were wed.

"Sit up, sweetheart."

I did as he bid and moved to sit in the middle of the bed. Wiley sat on the side and opened the jar. "Here, dip your fingers in."

I slipped two fingers into the cool, slippery substance and held them up.

"Rub your fingers over your nipple."

I looked down at my tight tips and took it between my slick digits. "Oh," I gasped.

Glancing up at Wiley, he was grinning, dipping his own fingers into the ointment. "Rub it in, make that nipple nice and slick. Good. Now dip the fingers from your other hand in and do the same with your other nipple."

I complied readily, soon playing with my slippery little nubs. It was so different than touching them when they were dry. Now, my fingers slipped right over the sensitive flesh.

"See how that lubricant feels? That's what it's going to be like when my fingers and cock are on your ass, slipping inside."

He took his shirt from the floor and wiped first one of my hands, then the other so they weren't so slick.

"Up on your knees and grab hold of the headboard."

I moved into position and looked over my shoulder at him. He came up onto his knees behind me, scooped up my long hair and slipped it over my shoulder, then caressed down the line of my spine. Goose flesh rose on my arms and I shivered at the light contact.

Instead of sliding his hand back up again, he dipped it directly between the part in my bottom to brush over my back entrance. His touch was cool and slick.

He moved even closer so that I felt his warm back against mine, the hairs on his chest tickling me. Kisses were pressed into the line of my shoulder.

As his finger began to circle and rim my entrance, his other hand cupped my breast, playing with the distended, glistening tip.

The combination was very intense, the ointment provided a different level of sensation. I tilted my head back so it rested against his shoulder, my fingers barely holding onto the metalwork of the headboard.

Wiley pinched my nipple and I gasped. Right then, he forged ahead with his finger in my ass and was able to push past my fighting ring of muscle. I groaned at the feel of being stretched open. It burned slightly, but the ointment made his finger so slippery that it was able to slide in effortlessly.

"There." Wiley gently bit the tendon where my neck

joined my shoulder, which had me jolting and clenching down on his fingertip.

"Oh!" I cried out. Relaxing allowed him to move in further, but clenching down had little bursts of heat course through me. My skin was slick with sweat, the ache in my pussy only intensifying because Wiley was completely neglecting it. My pussy felt empty and my clit pulsed with unfulfilled need.

Wiley started to move his finger, in and out, as if offering up a demonstration of what his cock would do there very soon. He slid in deeper and deeper until his finger was in all the way and his other fingers brushed over the entrance to my pussy and my clit. "Yes, please, Wiley."

"You need to come?"

I nodded my head against his shoulder, licked my lips.

"You need to come with my finger in your ass?"

"Yes!"

"Good girl." He expertly worked my clit and it didn't take more than a second or two to come, for he'd primed me well. It took just a simple touch and I was screaming, no doubt every hotel guest knew what we were up to, but I didn't care.

I didn't care about anything but how Wiley made me feel. He knew what would please me; in less than a week he was an expert on my body. As Wiley's fingers plucked at my nipple, I clenched down again and again on his finger buried within me. It felt *so* good, that after the pleasure ebbed, I wanted more.

His finger stilled within me and his hand moved away from my breast.

"Let go of the headboard, sweetheart and put your head on the pillow, ass in the air."

My grip was so damp I was relieved to let go. The pillow felt cool beneath my cheek and I sighed in this comfortable position, although his finger was still deep within me.

I watched as Wiley grabbed the base of his cock and lined himself up with my pussy, the blunt head nudging at my entrance.

"Let's get you all ready for me," he murmured, sinking into me slowly, yet surely. It was a tight fit with both his cock and finger inside. I was more than ready for him, my pussy dripping with my need.

I groaned as he bottomed out, his balls slapping against my sensitive clit.

He began to move his cock in time with his finger, fucking me slowly.

I heard Wiley's deep breathing, felt his tight grip on my hip. I wasn't the only one affected.

"It feels so good," I said. I may have lied in the past to protect him, but I would never lie about this. I would never lie about how he made me feel.

"You're going to make me come again, Piper, but this time I want to spend in your ass. I want to mark you there."

The heated words had me relaxing and softening, allowing him to slide in even remarkably deeper. Wiley pulled his cock all the way out and I cried out my disappointment. I felt empty and needy and so close to coming. Was he being intentionally cruel?

I looked over my shoulder and saw him dip his fingers in the jar of ointment, then spread the glistening substance over the length of his ruddy cock. It was so big, so swollen, almost angry looking. It must have taken much energy for him to pull out.

Once complete, he carefully slipped his finger from my ass and I immediately felt his cock there, then begin to push forward, then ease up.

"Relax, sweetheart. Take a deep breath, good. Now let it out and relax. Push back for me."

His cock was so slippery that when I did as he said, the broad head of his cock stretched me wide, then slid in. I could have sworn I heard a 'pop' but it was just in my mind, for that's what it felt like.

We both groaned together. Wiley dropped to brace himself on one hand, his chest curving over my back. In this position, he was able to slowly move forward and back, filling me a little at a time.

It was so much different than his cock in my pussy; so much tighter, with a hint of pain, yet so much more intense.

I could feel my orgasm just out of reach, for the feelings within my pussy where he'd stroked to life, combined with finding all kinds of new sensitive places deep within my ass had me on the brink.

"I need to come, Wiley. Please, oh God, let me come."

His breath fanned my shoulder, his kisses almost wild. His teeth even nipped along my shoulder. It was as if he were a stallion marking me.

"Touch yourself, sweetheart. Rub you clit and fly."

I didn't delay, but reached down between my legs and touched myself. I'd come so recently that I just had to flick over that engorged little bud and I came, this time my scream lodged in my throat.

"Jesus, you're strangling my dick. I can't hold back," Wiley growled and in one last thrust of his hips, he bit down on my shoulder and I felt the torrent of hot seed filling me.

It was the most intense orgasm ever and when it ebbed, I had nothing left. I was so sated, so well satisfied I all but wilted into the bed.

Wiley slowly pulled from me and I felt his hot seed slip out with him.

"That's a gorgeous sight." Wiley's possessiveness was apparent and very appealing.

I smiled into the pillow. "Mmm," I replied. "I feel very well cared for."

Wiley dropped down beside me so we faced each other. "Cared for? That's what you have to say about the best fuck of my life? Your life, I'll have you know." He almost sounded grumpy about my description.

"As I said before, I don't have much to go by, therefore you will need to continue to prove yourself."

He flopped onto his back and threw his arm over his eyes. "Woman, you're going to be the death of me."

"Let's do it again," I replied wickedly. I felt as if I was finally free and Wiley was my partner in life, my partner in fucking.

"A bath. We need a bath and then I'll do as you bid. I will be your stallion and service you just as you need. All day long. Once we get home to the ranch, I won't let you out of bed."

I rolled onto my belly so I lay half on top of him and toyed with the hair on his chest.

"Mmm. I like the idea of being serviced, and the idea of going home even more, but do you think we can work on that baby?"

He pulled his arm away and looked at me with those piercing green eyes. "Anything you say, sweetheart. Anything you say."

But I won't claim her alone. Jed Cassidy and I share everything, and that includes her. If the sweet little librarian isn't ready to be wrangled by two rodeo champs, we'll just have to break her in nice and slow. She's ours. We will win her over—body and soul—and when we do? Well, let's just say we'll give her a hard ride...and it'll last a hell of a lot longer than eight seconds.

Kaitlyn Leary takes one look at the sexy cowboys and can't remember the last time she was so eager for a double helping of... big beef. But giving in to desire might ruin everything. Because the truth is that this small town librarian isn't all she seems. Landon Duke and Jed might be talking about a future of picket fences and making babies, but the past could destroy it all. Still...two cowboys?

Who could resist?

NOTE FROM VANESSA

Guess what? I've got some bonus content for you! Sign up for my mailing list. There will be special bonus content for some of my books, just for my subscribers. Signing up will let you hear about my next release as soon as it is out, too (and you get a free book...wow!)

As always...thanks for loving my books and the wild ride!

JOIN THE WAGON TRAIN!

If you're on Facebook, please join my closed group, the Wagon Train! Don't miss out on the giveaways and hot cowboys!

https://www.facebook.com/groups/vanessavalewagontrain/

GET A FREE BOOK!

Join my mailing list to be the first to know of new releases, free books, special prices and other author giveaways.

http://freeromanceread.com

ALSO BY VANESSA VALE

Wolf Ranch Series

Rough

Wild

Feral

Savage

Wild Mountain Men

Mountain Darkness

Mountain Delights

Mountain Desire

Mountain Danger

Grade-A Beefcakes

Sir Loin Of Beef

T-Bone

Tri-Tip

Porterhouse

Skirt Steak

Small Town Romance

Montana Fire

Montana Ice

Montana Heat

Montana Wild

Montana Mine

Steele Ranch

Spurred

Wrangled

Tangled

Hitched

Lassoed

Bridgewater County Series

Ride Me Dirty

Claim Me Hard

Take Me Fast

Hold Me Close

Make Me Yours

Kiss Me Crazy

Mail Order Bride of Slate Springs Series

A Wanton Woman

A Wild Woman

A Wicked Woman

Bridgewater Ménage Series

Their Runaway Bride

Their Kidnapped Bride

Their Wayward Bride

Their Captivated Bride

Their Treasured Bride

Their Christmas Bride

Their Reluctant Bride

Their Stolen Bride

Their Brazen Bride

Their Rebellious Bride

Their Reckless Bride

Outlaw Brides Series

Flirting With The Law

MMA Fighter Romance Series

Fight For Her

Lenox Ranch Cowboys Series

Cowboys & Kisses

Spurs & Satin

Reins & Ribbons

Brands & Bows

Lassos & Lace

Montana Men Series

The Lawman

The Cowboy

The Outlaw

Standalone Reads

Twice As Delicious

Bride Pact

Sweet Justice

Mine To Take

Relentless

Sleepless Night

Man Candy - A Coloring Book

ABOUT THE AUTHOR

Vanessa Vale is the *USA Today* bestselling author of sexy romance novels, including her popular Bridgewater historical series and hot contemporary romances. With over one million books sold, Vanessa writes about unapologetic bad boys who don't just fall in love, they fall hard. Her books are available worldwide in multiple languages in e-book, print, audio and even as an online game. When she's not writing, Vanessa savors the insanity of raising two boys and figuring out how many meals she can make with a pressure cooker. While she's not as skilled at social media as her kids, she loves to interact with readers.

www.vanessavaleauthor.com

Instagram

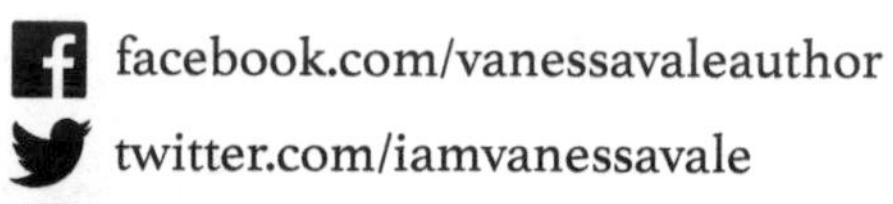

facebook.com/vanessavaleauthor

twitter.com/iamvanessavale

instagram.com/vanessa_vale_author

bookbub.com/profile/vanessa-vale